RELICS *of* REDEMPTION

Relics of Redemption

ISBN: 979-8-9893424-4-0 (hardback)
979-8-9893424-6-4 (paperback)

Printed in the United States of America

RELICS *of* REDEMPTION

A Jeannie Loomis Novel
with Sean Delaney

GARY J. ROSE

For my parents,

the hero and heroine of my life……

ACKNOWLEDGEMENTS

I would like to extend my heartfelt gratitude to my sister, Debbie Rose Miller, for her invaluable contribution to this project. Debbie's meticulous review of the initial manuscript uncovered errors and omissions that had escaped my notice, a testament to her unwavering support. I am certain that our mother would be immensely proud of her dedication.

I also want to express my sincere appreciation to Gillian McDonald. Her exceptional editing skills and insightful recommendations played a pivotal role in propelling the Jeannie Loomis novels into the upper echelons of the thriller and adventure genre on Amazon. Without Gillian's expertise, this achievement would not have been possible.

RELICS OF REDEMPTION

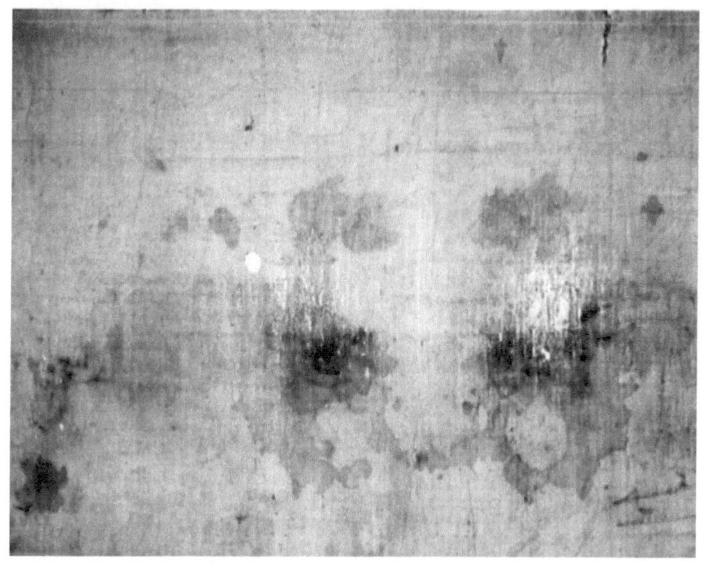

The Sudarium of Oviedo, or Shroud of Oviedo

The relic of the true cross St. Helena brought to Rome from the Holy Land

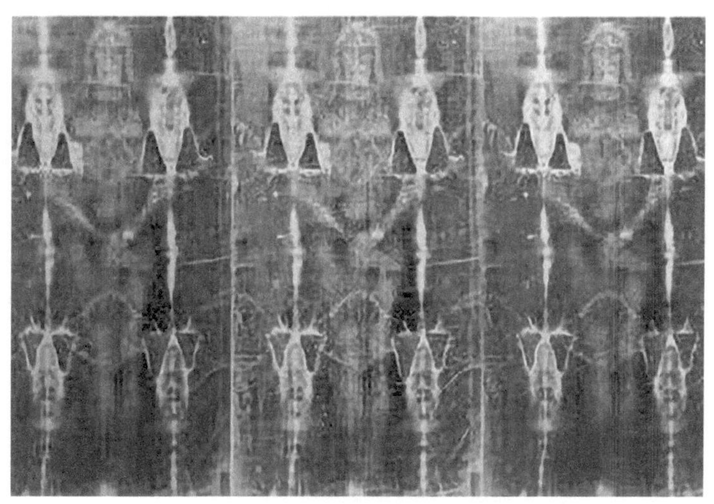

The Shroud of Turin

Not every relic that is above all doubt must be false.

—Hippolyte Delehaye

HISTORICAL BACKGROUND

Within the pages of this fictional novel, we delve into the life of complex yet unwavering law enforcement officer FBI agent Jeannie Loomis, and explore a profound theme—relics. These are not just any relics, but rather, sacred artifacts imbued with religious significance from bygone eras. Typically, relics consist of physical remains or personal possessions of saints or revered individuals, preserved to serve as tangible memorials for veneration.

This narrative centers in particular on the two most renowned relics associated with Jesus Christ of Nazareth, a central figure in Christianity. According to biblical accounts, Jesus was the Son of God, born to the Virgin Mary, and he endured suffering and death at the hands of Pontius Pilate. He was crucified, laid to rest in a tomb, and, as Christian doctrine maintains, transcended death, ascending to his Father in heaven after three days.

These relics hold a special place in the hearts of Christian believers and even captivate the curiosity of those who cherish history, prompting the question,

"What are these relics, and why are they of such profound importance to the Christian faith?"

The Sudarium of Oviedo, also known as the Shroud of Oviedo, is a precious relic safeguarded by the cathedral in the town of Oviedo in the northern region of Spain. This revered artifact is a piece of cloth measuring approximately 84 by 53 centimeters (33.7 inches by 28.9 inches). Unlike the Shroud of Turin, which bears an image, the Sudarium reveals no discernible picture to the naked eye, though microscopic examinations unveil more intricate details. What renders this cloth remarkable is the compelling blend of tradition and scientific scrutiny, both of which assert that it was employed to enshroud and protect a momentous relic—the face of Jesus Christ himself.

The other relic is the Shroud of Turin. This relic is a length of linen cloth that bears a faint image of the front and back of a man. It measures 4.4m by 1.1m or 14'5" by 3'7". It has been venerated for centuries, especially by members of the Catholic Church, as the actual burial shroud used to wrap the body of Jesus of Nazareth after his crucifixion, and upon which Jesus's bodily image is miraculously imprinted.

Such a cloth is known to have existed from the gospel of John, chapter 20, verses 6 and 7. These verses read as follows: "Simon Peter, following him, also came up, went into the tomb, saw the linen cloth lying on the ground, and also the cloth that had been over his head; this was not with the linen cloth but rolled up in a place by itself." John clearly differentiates between this smaller face cloth, the Sudarium, and the larger linen that wrapped the body.

The Sudarium's history is meticulously documented, offering a more straightforward narrative compared to the enigmatic tale of the Shroud of Turin. Primary sources trace back to Pelagius (Pelayo), the twelfth-century bishop of Oviedo, whose historical works, the Book of the Testaments of Oviedo and the Chronicon Regum Legionensium, unveil the Sudarium's journey.

According to historical accounts, the Sudarium resided in Palestine until 614 when Chosroes II, the Persian king, invaded and conquered Jerusalem. Fearing destruction, the presbyter Philip transported the relic to Alexandria, then across North Africa as Chosroes' forces overtook Alexandria in 616.

Eventually reaching Cartagena in Spain alongside refugees fleeing the Persian onslaught, the Sudarium found sanctuary under the benevolent eye of Bishop Fulgentius of Ecija. It was then entrusted to Leandro, Bishop of Seville, and found a temporary home in Seville.

In contrast, the Shroud of Turin's historical ownership is murkier, but modern science has invested countless hours in meticulous study and research, making it the most scrutinized artifact in human history.

The Shroud, now housed in Turin Cathedral, lacks clear historical records before the 14th century. While a burial cloth, possibly the Shroud, was once in possession of Byzantine emperors, it vanished during the Sack of Constantinople in 1204. Reports of veneration for Jesus' burial Shroud or an image of his head existed before the 14th century, but no conclusive evidence ties them to the Turin Shroud.

Historical records suggest the appearance of a crucified man's image on a shroud in Lirey, France, around 1353 to 1357. Owned by French knight Geoffroi de Charny, who perished at the Battle of Poitiers in 1356, the shroud faced skepticism from Bishop Pierre d'Arcis in 1390. The bishop, asserting forgery, claimed a predecessor had identified the artist.

From the 15th century, the Shroud's history is well-documented. In 1453, Margaret de Charny transferred ownership to the House of Savoy. In 1532, a fire in Chambéry damaged the shroud, and efforts by Poor Clare Nuns to repair it left distinct marks. In 1578, Duke Emmanuel Philibert of Savoy relocated the cloth from Chambéry to Turin, where it has remained ever since.

The most esteemed artifact, perhaps best described as the True Cross, is believed to be the actual cross upon which Jesus of Nazareth was crucified, according to Christian tradition. Numerous historical records and legends recount how Helena, the mother of Roman Emperor Constantine the Great, journeyed to the Holy Land between 326 and 328 AD. She is said to have discovered the True Cross during her visit to the Holy Sepulchre in Jerusalem.

One of these crosses bore the inscription with Jesus' name, and while Helena initially had doubts about its authenticity, a miracle is said to have confirmed that it was, indeed, the True Cross. This event is commemorated in the liturgical calendar as the Feast of the Exaltation of the Cross by various Christian denominations, including the Oriental Orthodox, Eastern Orthodox, Persian, Roman Catholic, Lutheran, and Anglican Churches.

The Roman Catholic Church, Eastern Orthodox Church, Oriental Orthodox Church, and the Church of the East all lay claim to possessing relics associated with the True Cross, which they hold in reverence. In contrast, Protestant and some other Christian denominations generally dispute the authenticity of these relics and do not regard them as highly significant.

As we journey through the pages of this novel, we shall unravel the enigma surrounding these relics, exploring their profound significance to the Christian faith and their potential to unearth secrets that could forever alter our understanding of history and spirituality.

During her sojourn, as documented by the annals of late 4th-century historians such as Gelasius of Caesarea and Tyrannius Rufinus, Helena unveiled a cryptic secret concealed within the annals of time—a trio of crosses purportedly employed in the crucifixion of Jesus and his fellow transgressors, Dismas and Gestas. These crosses held within them a profound enigma, cloaked in the mists of antiquity. Among them, one bore a titulus inscribed with the name of Jesus, yet Helena harbored doubts about its authenticity.

It was through an extraordinary twist of fate, a miracle witnessed by those in her entourage, that the divine nature of this cross, the True Cross, was unveiled. The very moment of revelation has since been etched into the liturgical calendars of diverse Christian traditions, celebrated as the Feast of the Exaltation of the Cross, often known as Roodmas. This grand commemoration is observed with reverence by Oriental Orthodox, Eastern Orthodox, Persian, Roman Catholic, Lutheran, and Anglican congregations.

Church of the Holy Sepulchre

CHAPTER ONE

The night was heavy with the promise of secrets as the moon hung low in the sky, casting its eerie glow upon the ancient city of Oviedo. Nestled amid rolling hills and bathed in history, Oviedo was a place where the past intertwined seamlessly with the present. Its streets, paved with cobblestones smoothed by the footsteps of centuries, had borne witness to tales of heroes and legends, but none were as storied as the relic housed within the heart of its sacred temple.

Tall, ornate spires pierced the night sky, their intricate architecture illuminated by the soft radiance of lamplights that lined the winding streets. Oviedo, in the north of Spain, had always been a city of mystery, its labyrinthine alleyways and hidden courtyards holding untold secrets.

The temple that guarded the Sodarium was a masterpiece of ancient design. Its massive bronze doors, adorned with intricate carvings depicting scenes of redemption and salvation, stood as testaments to the city's deep spiritual roots. The walls surrounding the temple were built from the same ancient stone that had withstood centuries of turmoil, their surfaces worn smooth by time.

Vines and ivy crept up the walls, their tendrils weaving a tapestry of life around the sacred structure. As Vincent D'Amico stood just outside the temple, he couldn't help but marvel at the juxtaposition of beauty and danger that Oviedo presented. For centuries, this place had guarded a relic of immeasurable power, a source of hope and salvation known as the Sodarium of Oviedo. Soon, that would all change.

Hidden within the depths of the city's most sacred temple, the Sodarium was a legend whispered about through the ages. It was said to possess the ability to heal the most grievous wounds, to resurrect the dying, and to bring redemption to those who sought it. For many, it was a symbol of faith, but for one man, it was an object of unfathomable desire.

Vincent's gloved hand clutched the temple's blueprints, his fingers tracing the intricate pathways leading to the relic's chamber. He had bribed and deceived where he could and eliminated anyone who posed a threat to his operation. The temple's security guards were on his payroll, and the city's surveillance system had been tampered with, leaving him with a blind spot right where he needed it.

His earpiece crackled to life, and a low voice whispered, "Vincent, we're in position. The guards are on their rounds, and the cameras are down. It's now or never." Vincent nodded, his heart pounding in his chest. The heist of the century was about to begin.

Silently, he slipped through the shadows and approached the massive bronze doors. His gloved hand reached for the concealed panel, and he entered the security code, a sequence he had obtained through a web of informants and blackmail. The heavy doors creaked open, revealing a dimly lit corridor.

With each step, Vincent felt the weight of centuries of history pressing down on him. The air was thick with the scent of ancient incense, and the walls were adorned with faded frescoes depicting long-forgotten tales of redemption and sacrifice.

As Vincent moved deeper into the temple, his crew followed closely behind. Each member of his team was handpicked for their unique skills. There was Elara, the master locksmith, and Andrei, the tech genius who could hack into any system. And then there was Natalia, the Russian beauty, the acrobat, who could navigate even the most treacherous of obstacles.

The tension in the air was thick as they approached the relic's chamber. Vincent knew any misstep now could lead to disaster. He could almost taste the Sodarium's power, so close yet still out of reach.

Suddenly, a soft voice echoed through the corridor, sending shivers down Vincent's spine, "Who goes there?" He froze, his heart thumping as he turned to see a robed figure emerging from the shadows, a guardian of the temple, armed with a staff adorned with glowing runes. Someone who had apparently not been paid off.

Time seemed to stand still as the two men locked eyes in a silent battle of wills. The fate of his daring heist hung in the balance as the relic of redemption remained tantalizingly close, but just out of reach.

Vincent and the guardian stood in a chilling standoff. Every heartbeat reverberated like a drumroll announcing impending doom. The cold sweat trickled down Vincent's temple, and the guardian's eyes bore into him with an unwavering resolve.

Without a moment's hesitation, Natalia, her lithe form shrouded in the shadows until now, stepped forward. In her gloved hand, she cradled a .22 caliber semi-automatic with a suppressor. It was a weapon as lethal as it was discreet, chosen for its ability to maintain the sacred silence of their covert operation.

In an instant, the hushed tranquility of the temple was shattered as the suppressed gunshot echoed through the corridor. The silenced bullet found its mark with deadly precision, striking the temple guard in the forehead. His eyes widened in a brief moment of shock before life escaped him, leaving his lifeless body to crumple to the cold stone floor.

With the body of the temple guardian laying behind them, Vincent and his team pressed on through the labyrinthine corridors. Their footsteps were muffled by the thick carpets that adorned the ancient stone floors, and the flickering candlelight cast eerie shadows, making the temple seem like a realm suspended between the worlds of the living and the divine.

Their target, the Sodarium of Oviedo, lay in the innermost sanctum of the temple—a chamber shrouded in darkness and guarded by an intricate network of traps, both mystical and mechanical. The legend surrounding the relic spoke of its immense power, and Vincent knew the security measures in place would also be nothing short of legendary.

When they reached the grand chamber's entrance, a colossal bronze door adorned with religious symbols stood before them. Vincent held his breath. The portal was a feat of ancient engineering and unlocking its secrets had been one of the greatest challenges in their meticulous planning.

Elara, the master locksmith, stepped forward, her nimble fingers working deftly. She inserted a set of specially crafted tools into the intricate lock mechanism. The tumblers clicked softly, and with a triumphant twist, the massive door began to groan open.

With agonizing slowness, the bronze portal revealed the chamber within. It was bathed in a soft, otherworldly glow, emanating from the relic itself—a radiant tapestry of light woven from the hopes and prayers of countless generations.

The Sodarium rested on a pedestal of polished marble, encased in a glass dome that sparkled with an almost ethereal shimmer. Its surface bore markings of celestial script, telling the tale of its creation, and its aura pulsed with an energy that sent shivers down their spines.

Vincent's heart raced as he gazed upon the relic, his hand trembling with anticipation. He could almost taste the power it held, the redemption it promised to those who possessed it. Yet, this final step was fraught with peril.

Andrei, the tech genius, approached the security panel next to the relic. With swift precision, he began to disable the last line of defense. It was a complex array of sensors and alarms, a digital fortress guarding the relic. Sweat formed on his brow as he worked, and every passing second felt like an eternity.

Natalia stood at the ready, her acrobatic skills honed to perfection. She would be the one to retrieve the relic once the security was fully disabled. Her lithe form and impeccable balance made her the ideal candidate for this task, and her eyes never left the glass dome that held the Sodarium.

As the final alarm was disarmed, a sigh of relief swept through the team. The temple was silent, as though holding its breath, waiting for the moment of truth.

In one fluid, graceful motion, Natalia leaped onto the pedestal, her gloved hands enveloping the glass dome. With a gentle twist, the dome released, and she carefully cradled the Sodarium in her hands. Its radiant light bathed her in a warm glow and, for a moment, it seemed as though time itself had stopped.

The relic was theirs, a prize more valuable than any they had ever stolen, and as they retreated from the chamber, the weight of their daring heist permeated the air. Their mission was complete, but the true challenges lay ahead, for the power of the Sodarium of Oviedo had the potential to shape their destinies in ways they could only begin to imagine.

CHAPTER TWO

Jeannie's eyes snapped open, and she was greeted by a familiar, unwelcome throbbing in her temples. It was the kind of headache that made even the softest rustle of sheets sound like a thunderous symphony. Groaning softly, she turned her gaze to her alarm clock as its luminous digits pierced the predawn darkness announcing 4:10 a.m.

"Ugh," she muttered to the empty room, her voice a hoarse whisper that betrayed her frustration. The morning hours were mercilessly indifferent to her discomfort. She knew, from long experience, that sleep would remain an elusive dream.

Jeannie tossed and turned, seeking refuge in the embrace of sleep, but it seemed that slumber had abandoned her for the night. Her irritation mounted as her attempts to return to any stage of sleep proved utterly futile. The room remained silent, save for the muffled ticking of the clock, counting down the inexorable march of time.

With a resigned sigh she kicked her covers back revealing her modest attire—a SF 49er's t-shirt and well-worn gray sweatpants. Her long, tousled blond hair cascaded over her pillowcase, forming a golden halo around her head. It was an image that suggested her most recent investigation—the one the media called 'Snow Angel.'

In the dim glow of her bedroom, Jeannie's mind drifted back to that chilling case. The memory was as vivid as if it had happened only yesterday. The victim, a woman found in the unforgiving embrace of winter's snow, had haunted her thoughts ever since. Even though she had not visited the crime scene, the photos shared with her from the Idaho State Police had made a lasting impression.

The victim had been lying face up, her body nestled in the pristine snow like a macabre work of art, but what had sent a shiver down Jeannie's spine was the way the woman's long, ebony hair had fanned out around her head, creating an eerie, angelic tableau.

The sight had been both haunting and mesmerizing, etching itself into Jeannie's memory like a dark stain on her psyche. It was the kind of image that never quite faded, no matter how many cases she solved or how many sleepless nights she spent wrestling with the demons of her profession. The Snow Angel's visage, with her long ebony hair splayed out over the snow, seemed to follow Jeannie, even in the dim corners of her mind.

What made it worse was the sinister backdrop against which that haunting tableau had been painted. It had marked the beginning of her relentless pursuit of an elusive serial killer whose sinister web spanned several western states. His kills had stretched into double digits, leaving a trail of fear, grief, and unanswered questions behind that scarred entire communities.

Jeannie shuddered as she remembered the mounting body count and the unsettling realization that each victim had fallen prey to the same meticulous predator. The perpetrator had displayed a chilling ability to vanish into the shadows, leaving no trace of his presence beyond the lifeless bodies he left behind. The relentlessness of his crimes, the calculated nature of his killings, and the macabre rituals that tied them together had all pointed to a man who reveled in darkness.

It had taken every ounce of Jeannie's determination, intuition, and investigative prowess to finally close in on him. The pursuit had been grueling, fraught with false leads and dead ends that tested her resolve. But Jeannie had pushed forward, driven by a fierce determination to bring justice to the victims and their grieving families.

The night she had finally cornered the serial killer had brought a relentless game of cat and mouse. He had tried to elude her one last time, slipping through alleys and disappearing into the night, but she had been one step ahead. The final confrontation had been a tense, heart-pounding battle of wits and nerve, a moment that had left its indelible mark on Jeannie's memory. And she had delivered justice to the suspect when, from out of the blue, hair fibers from one of his victims were found in the truck he had recently driven.

As she continued to lay in her sleepless state, the memory of that chilling pursuit came rushing back, intertwining with the image of the Snow Angel. It was a reminder of the darkness that lurked in the corners of the world and the unyielding dedication it took to confront it. Jeannie's journey had been one of sacrifice, determination, and an unshakable commitment to protecting those who couldn't protect themselves.

For some inexplicable reason, the memories of her team's previous case merged seamlessly with visions of the Snow Angel before taking control of her thoughts. That case had revolved around the last remaining clone generated from the remains of Adolph Hitler, who had mysteriously vanished after their involvement in a prior mission concerning a clandestine group known as The Organization. The shadowy syndicate comprised modern-day Nazis who harbored ambitions of resurrecting a Fourth Reich on a global scale.

The returning clone, with cunning manipulation, ascended to the highest echelons of the German government, ultimately becoming the Chancellor of Germany. With The Organization's tentacles extending across the globe, the world appeared to teeter on the brink of perilous dominion. Thankfully, an anonymous sniper intervened, extinguishing his dreams of world conquest. As Jeannie and her team closed in on the cloned Hitler, his henchmen retaliated.

A vivid memory emerged – the horrifying bombing attempt by The Organization at her home. The blast had shattered the tranquility of her once-idyllic abode and wreaked havoc on her prized possession, a luxurious $150,000 Corvette meticulously housed in the garage. It was a traumatic incident that could have cost her life, but fate had something else in store.

Miraculously, the saving grace had come in the form of a fire door that connected the garage to her kitchen. This unassuming door had acted as a formidable shield, successfully dissipating the explosion's force. Thanks to this stroke of luck, she emerged unscathed from the harrowing incident, her life spared.

Fast forward to the present and she found herself comfortably seated in the recently constructed garage, which was now home to her latest automotive obsession – a dazzling, fire engine red Ferrari F8. The gleaming beauty of her new acquisition stood in stark contrast to the grim memories of the past. It was a symbol of resilience and a testament to her unwavering determination to rise above adversity. Yes, a little frivolous, but with the inheritance from her recently discovered mother, the cost of the automobile was nothing.

The saleswoman who facilitated the purchase of this high-end sports car couldn't hide her astonishment when Jeannie nonchalantly declined any financing options and chose to settle the entire bill with cold, hard cash. Some might have deemed this decision impractical, given the substantial sum of money involved. However, Jeannie had her own rationale.

Impractical? Perhaps, but for Jeannie, life was too short to be solely governed by practicality. She firmly believed that if you had the means and had worked tirelessly to achieve your goals, there was nothing wrong with indulging in a little extravagance and seizing opportunities to savor the finer things in life.

For Jeannie, her new Ferrari F8 wasn't just a car; it was a symbol of her unwavering spirit and a tangible representation of the motto she lived by, "If you have the money, and you work hard, why not have some fun?"

Jeannie saw no need for a bathrobe that Saturday morning. With the weekend stretching out before her like an open book, she relished the idea of the leisurely hours ahead. The only appointment on her agenda was the four o'clock mass at St. Edwards, a weekly ritual she held dear. Other than that, her day was a canvas waiting to be filled with the colors of relaxation and indulgence.

The soft morning light filtered through her bedroom window as she moved about the house in her comfortable t-shirt and pajama bottoms.

In her role as the Assistant Special Agent in Charge of the San Francisco FBI bureau, Jeannie assumed all the duties and responsibilities associated with her title. Her supervisor, SAC Lomax, significantly enhanced her job experience by recognizing Jeannie's passion for leading major investigations with her team, rather than burdening her with what she considered to be unnecessary bureaucratic paperwork.

Together with her team, she had successfully resolved numerous significant investigations, one of which led to a presidential award ceremony where she stood alongside her partner, friend, and trusted confidant, FBI agent Ismail Flores.

Downstairs, in the dining room, her prized koi swam gracefully in a large aquarium. Their vibrant colors and elegant movements were sources of endless fascination for Jeannie. The tank was a living masterpiece, a slice of tranquility that she cherished. She often found herself lost in their world, the rhythmic dance of the koi providing a soothing backdrop to her thoughts.

Beyond the glass walls of her dining room, a haven awaited her in the form of a meticulously designed Japanese garden. Its centerpiece was a koi pond, a shimmering oasis of serenity. The pond was a labor of love, a testament to her dedication to creating a sanctuary of beauty and peace.

Jeannie shared a profound bond with her koi that reached deep into her soul. Their resilience and the graceful way they faced life's obstacles had always struck a chord with her. They were qualities she aspired to embody in her life, particularly in the relentless world of darkness she confronted in her line of work.

Their aquatic world reflected the strength and poise she yearned for. However, life had a way of unveiling unexpected connections. The revelation had come as a delightful surprise when she discovered that her recently found biological mother, who hailed from Myrtle Beach, South Carolina, shared a similar passion for nurturing her own enchanting garden. The place had been bequeathed to Jeannie as a tangible legacy from her newfound family.

As the morning sun warmed her skin, Jeannie ventured outside into her Japanese garden. The koi, aware of her presence, swam to the surface, their scales catching the sunlight. She sat on the wooden bridge that arched gracefully over the pond, which was a place of reflection and solace.

The world around her seemed to slow down as she watched the koi glide beneath the water's surface. Their movements were a reminder of the simple joys of life, the beauty that could be found even in the most tranquil moments. This was her oasis, her sanctuary, somewhere she could recharge her spirit and find solace before the world outside beckoned her back into its complex realities.

As Jeannie continued to nurture her koi pond, she couldn't help but feel the presence of her biological mother, even though they had never met. In the gentle, swishing movements of the koi she discerned a connection that transcended time and distance. It was as if the essence of her mother's spirit lived on in the tranquil waters of both their gardens, reminding Jeannie that, despite the challenges and darkness of the past, there was a deep wellspring of beauty and resilience to draw strength from.

Upon receiving the news of her biological mother's passing, Jeannie discovered that she had inherited a substantial fortune, including property in Myrtle Beach. This necessitated her journey to the area to meet with her mother's estate attorney. The magnitude of her mother's wealth was in the millions. With no remaining family of her own, Jeannie generously gifted one of her mother's ocean-view high-rise apartments to her mother's dedicated, long-time caregiver and housekeeper. She also arranged for a monthly stipend to ensure the house's ongoing care, including her mother's beloved black cat, Missy.

Over the years following her change in fortune, Jeannie would occasionally make trips to Myrtle Beach to enjoy the expansive estate and her mother's magnificent vintage Victorian Edwardian botanical conservatory sunroom. She would spend hours in this lush haven, and she even found herself napping at times amid the vibrant greenery beside the Japanese koi pond and the melodious chorus of numerous waterfalls. It was a cherished connection to her mother.

CHAPTER THREE

The castle appeared to belong to a distant past, with its colossal stone structure showcasing exquisite craftsmanship. Surprisingly, the castle's origins only traced back to the late 20th century. Nestled along the Northeast coast of Spain, boasting breathtaking views of the Mediterranean Sea, it was fully constructed in 1994. The castle stood out as one of the finest examples of modern-era castles in the country. Its architectural design paid homage to Roman, Byzantine, Gothic, and Middle Eastern influences from the medieval period.

Vincent D'Amico spared no expense in overseeing his castle's construction. He insisted on employing only the most skilled craftsmen and artisans, and left no room for compromise when it came to the selection of premium construction materials. The finest woods and exquisite trims were carefully selected to ensure every detail reflected the utmost in quality and luxury. The construction stood as a testament to his unwavering commitment to excellence and opulence in every facet of its creation. It included false passages, hidden rooms, and, of course, a dungeon where in an environmentally controlled room, he housed his latest possession.

The master thief did not waste his ill-gotten wealth; instead, he relished flaunting it before his guests, most of whom were part of the upper echelons of society. Vincent D'Amico was a complex character with a multifaceted persona.

On the surface, he appeared to be a charismatic and charming jetsetter, living a life of luxury and indulgence. He effortlessly embodied the image of a playboy, easily moving through high-society circles and leaving a trail of admirers in his wake. His impeccable taste in fashion, fine dining, and exotic destinations only added to his allure.

However, beneath this glamorous façade lay a dangerous narcissist. Vincent was driven by an insatiable thirst for accumulating wealth and power. He saw himself as the center of the universe and believed everyone should be at his beck and call. His conscience seemed non-existent, as he was willing to eliminate anyone who dared to stand in his way or threaten his ambitions.

Vincent D'Amico's used his charm and manipulation skills to exploit others for personal gain.

He was a master of subterfuge, capable of weaving intricate webs of deceit to achieve his objectives. His moral compass was severely skewed, and he viewed people as mere pawns in his grand game of acquisition and dominance.

He descended the staircase to the dungeon with measured steps. Gas-fed lamps, designed to resemble torches from a bygone era, flickered as he advanced. The cold stone walls absorbed the warmth of his descent. Upon reaching the foot of the stone staircase, he faced an immense metal door with a digital keypad to its right.

He entered the correct code with precision, and the door opened slowly accompanied by a rush of air. Inside, he found himself in the first of two airlocks, waiting for the door behind him to seal shut before he could proceed to the final chamber. And there it was, displayed in a manner akin to the one in the Cathedral of San Salvador in Oviedo, Spain – the Sudarium of Oviedo.

The Sudarium, exhibiting advanced deterioration marked by symmetrically arranged yet imageless dark flecks, contrasted sharply with the distinct markings found on the Shroud of Turin. This face cloth's presence within the empty tomb was detailed in John 20:6–7. Beyond the biblical account, the earliest historical reference to the Sudarium dated to 570 A.D. when Antoninus of Piacenza mentioned its care in the vicinity of Jerusalem, specifically in a cave near the monastery of Saint Mark.

Vincent remained indifferent to the cloth's authenticity. To him, it merely represented a substantial deposit into one of his many offshore accounts in the Cayman Islands. His conscience remained untouched, even when dealing with those who had requested the Sudarium's theft, regardless of who they were or what they represented. However, he was convinced that he had deciphered their underlying motivations.

Jeannie, her morning routine a well-practiced symphony of flavors and aromas, effortlessly set her culinary wheels in motion. She deftly slid a handful of frozen French Toast slices into the waiting slots of her trusty toaster, each piece promising to transform into a golden, crispy delight. Meanwhile, in a sizzling pan, a trio of plump pork sausage links performed a sizzling ballet, their savory perfume wafting through the kitchen like a siren's call.

As the kitchen filled with the tantalizing scent of sizzling meat, Jeannie's faithful coffee maker hummed with purpose. It had dutifully executed its preprogrammed task, presenting her with a generous reservoir of liquid motivation in the form of ten cups of aromatic coffee. The rich, dark brew glistened enticingly in the pot; a promise of caffeinated bliss ready to accompany her morning feast.

Jeannie chose to keep her wooden shades firmly drawn intentionally, secretly harboring the hope of delaying an early morning visit from her friendly neighbors, Delores and Walter. She held a deep affection for the couple, but sometimes, their presence could be a tad overwhelming.

Delores and Walter were unwavering pillars in the realm of trustworthiness and honesty. Jeannie had grown accustomed to relying on them to safeguard her home during her frequent absences, entrusting them with the care of her finned companions and the responsibility of ensuring the weekly garbage pickup. They had proven themselves as steadfast guardians of her cherished abode, faithfully tending to its needs in her absence.

Despite their unwavering reliability and kindness, there were moments when Jeannie craved some solitude, a brief respite from the warmth of their companionship. Hence, the closed shades served as a gentle buffer, a shield of privacy designed not out of avoidance but rather a desire for a tranquil morning before she once more welcomed her dear neighbors into her world.

Jeannie's head began to spin and a wave of dizziness overcame her. She clung to her kitchen counter for support as the throbbing in her head intensified. After a few minutes, she started to feel a little better, except for the persistent headache. She then proceeded to butter her French Toast and serve her sausage.

"You know, maybe you're starting to get migraines," she mused to herself. "You're not getting any younger. Note to self: schedule an appointment with the doctor Monday."

As she powered on her television set, she carefully carried her plate of food over to her front room table, strategically positioning herself for the best view of the screen. Her choice of program today was Newsmax, and they were currently airing an intriguing international story about the theft of the Sodarium of Oviedo in Spain.

In a breaking announcement today, a Vatican representative confirmed the theft of the Sodarium of Oviedo, the cloth believed to have been used to cover the face of Jesus, from the Cathedral of San Salvador in Oviedo, Spain. Details surrounding the theft, including any involvement of Italian authorities, have not been disclosed by the Vatican at this time. We will stay tuned to this developing story for further updates.

Jeannie's fascination with relics, particularly the Sodarium of Oviedo, the Shroud of Turin, and the True Cross, stemmed from her undergraduate days when she had delved into the intriguing world of art history. Her professor had crafted a captivating lecture that intertwined these relics, and as she listened, a question began to form in Jeannie's mind. She couldn't help but wonder about the historical documentation that authenticated these revered artifacts.

The professor's response shed light on a compelling contrast. When it came to the Sodarium of Oviedo, a remarkable trail of documentation existed, chronicling its ownership history up to its current display in Oviedo. This rich historical record set it apart from the Shroud of Turin and the True Cross, where the scarcity of concrete evidence left room for doubt.

Jeannie's curiosity led her to inquire further, her devout Catholic upbringing propelling her to seek clarity regarding these relics associated with the life of Christ. Her professor elucidated the complex situation surrounding the Shroud of Turin.

It was initially discredited by some historians after carbon-14 dating placed it in the Middle Ages. However, subsequent investigations unveiled a fascinating twist. The piece of fabric used for the carbon-14 dating had been sewn onto the Shroud during the Middle Ages, concealing its true age. When another portion of the Shroud was examined, the results aligned with the crucifixion era, rekindling intrigue and debate.

This revelation exposed the intricate nature of relic authentication, where the story of each artifact wove a distinct narrative. While the Sodarium of Oviedo stood firm with its well-documented journey, the Shroud of Turin's path to validation had been a maze of discovery, with surprises hidden in its very fabric. And the only documentation regarding the True Cross is the pilgrimage to Jerusalem by St. Helena, where tradition claims she found Christ's true cross and built the Basilica of the Holy Sepulchre.

Jeannie's inquisitive nature had a way of sparking her inner investigator, even when the situation wasn't directly within her purview. As she contemplated the

Sodarium's audacious theft, her mind raced through a labyrinth of possibilities. Why would anyone target such a revered relic? The motives were as multifaceted as the machinations of history itself.

One of the first motives that sprang to mind was profit. The black market for stolen artifacts and religious relics was well-documented. The Sodarium, with its ancient lineage and deep spiritual significance, could fetch a hefty sum on the illicit market. Jeannie envisioned it passing through a shadowy network of collectors, each willing to pay a fortune for a piece of such significant history.

Another plausible scenario was the intention to hold the relic for ransom. Criminals often sought to exploit the emotional and spiritual significance of such items, knowing that the faithful would go to great lengths to secure their return. The Sodarium was not just a historical artifact; it also held a profound religious meaning for many, making it a prime target for ransom demands that could be both substantial and emotionally charged.

Jeannie couldn't help but feel a sense of intrigue building within her. The Sodarium's theft had morphed into an absorbing puzzle, one that called to her investigative instincts. It was, indeed, an interesting case – a tantalizing blend of history, spirituality, and criminality, where motives were as enigmatic as the artifact itself.

Her headache grew worse so she got an ice pack from the freezer and placed it on her forehead while lying on the couch, hoping Newsmax would return with more updated information.

CHAPTER FOUR

Jeannie's reverie dissolved with the gentle hum of her cell phone vibrating on the coffee table, pulling her back to the present. She couldn't help but grin as she glanced at the caller ID. It was her partner, Ismail Flores; a welcome interruption to her day.

As she picked up the call, a cheerful tone colored her voice. "Good morning, Ace. How's everything with you and the family on this sunny Saturday?"

Ismail's teasing banter was quick to follow, "Well, aren't you in a bright mood today? What's the occasion? Did you have a scintillating date last night? Is the charming gentleman still lingering around?"

The laughter that erupted from Ismail was so contagious that Jeannie had to stifle her response while conjuring a playful retort, "Oh, my goodness,

Ismail. You won't believe it. He was like a real-life superhero, a towering figure of a man. The moment I laid eyes on him he took my breath away. And when we went to bed, oh my God!"

Ismail chuckled heartily, his laugh resonating through the phone. Jeannie couldn't help but playfully counter as she embraced the jovial tone of their conversation. "You've got it all figured out, huh? But you're wrong this time. I did consider driving home after work, taking a relaxing shower, donning my comfy pajamas, and settling in front of the TV. You even guessed the delivery pizza part! But hey, who says a cozy night in can't be a delightful experience?"

Their light-hearted exchange continued, a testament to their enduring friendship and the bond that made them an exceptional team. Despite the mundane details of their daily lives, they found joy in the simple moments, sharing laughter and camaraderie that transcended the challenges they faced in their work as investigators.

"Hey, I'm calling because the wife wants to invite you over for dinner tonight. She's whipping up some mouthwatering shredded beef enchiladas, chili rellenos, and, to cap it all off, she's baked my all-time favorite devil's food chocolate cake paired with Rocky Road ice cream. Sound tempting?"

"Oh, my God, that menu sounds irresistible. Let her know that if I can shake this headache, I'll be there with bells on."

"Hey, boss, I couldn't help but notice that you've been having these headaches quite frequently. You know, as a highly-trained FBI agent, I've honed my skills in observing subtle nuances in human behavior, and I thought it was worth mentioning."

"Yes, Inspector Clouseau, I'm well aware of my headaches, and I've already made a mental note to call my doctor on Monday to schedule an appointment. I wouldn't be surprised if she tells me it's stress-related, given the demands of collaborating with a highly trained FBI agent! So, 5 p.m. it is. Thanks for the reminder, Ismail," Jeannie acknowledged with a hint of amusement in her tone. She appreciated her friend's straightforwardness, even if it came in the form of medical advice. As Ismail hung up, she couldn't help but chuckle at their easygoing rapport, knowing that her evening was already looking brighter with the prospect of dinner and good company.

As Saturday afternoon bathed the world in a warm, golden glow, Jeannie's spirits had noticeably improved. Feeling revitalized, she selected a tasteful pant suit from her wardrobe, slipping into it with a sense of purpose. Her destination was St. Edwards Church, a place that held special significance for her, thanks to a tradition initiated by her stepmother and stepfather.

Their custom was a rather pragmatic one – attending the Saturday afternoon mass. It had one distinct advantage, offering the promise of a peaceful Sunday morning lie-in. It was a practice her parents had established and, even though they were no longer with her, it was a tradition that Jeannie cherished as a connection to their memory.

On top of the convenience it provided, Jeannie had another reason to stick to this routine, especially during football season. With the San Francisco 49ers often gracing the television screen on Sundays, attending church on Saturdays allowed her to revel in the excitement of the games without missing a beat. As she made her way to the church, she reflected on the balance it brought to her life, combining her faith and her fondness for football, honoring tradition while forging her own path.

The choice of today's gospel couldn't have been more fitting. The priest's resonant voice filled the sacred space as he recited the verses from the Gospel of John 20:5-8. The timeless words, steeped in tradition and faith, hung in the air, finding a profound resonance in Jeannie's heart.

While the priest expounded on the ancient text, Jeannie's thoughts naturally gravitated toward the recent theft of the Sudarium relic that had been taken from its resting place. The words seemed to echo in her mind, intertwining with the mysteries surrounding the stolen artifact.

"And he, stooping down and looking in, saw the linen cloths lying there; yet he did not go in." Jeannie pondered how the thief might have approached the relic, almost hesitating to commit the act. The linen

cloths lay empty, much like the vault from which the Sudarium had disappeared.

"Then Simon Peter came, following him, and went into the tomb; and he saw the linen cloths lying there, and the handkerchief that had been around His head." The imagery of Peter investigating the tomb conjured the image of investigators delving into the case. The handkerchief, distinct from the linen cloths, sparked a parallel to the unique nature of the Sudarium itself, setting it apart from other relics.

"*Not lying with the linen cloths but folded together in a place by itself.*" The deliberate separation of the handkerchief, folded in solitude, mirrored the singular allure of the Sudarium, so unlike other sacred artifacts. Jeannie couldn't help but feel a sense of connection, as if the ancient scripture were guiding her in her pursuit of the truth.

"*Then the other disciple, who came to the tomb first, went in also; and he saw and believed.*" These closing words held a glimmer of hope, the possibility of belief after witnessing something remarkable. Jeannie held onto this glimmer, believing that, in the end, the truth about the stolen Sudarium would be revealed. As the gospel concluded and the congregation bowed their heads in prayer, Jeannie continued to seek guidance from the timeless words, interweaving the past and present in her quest for answers.

Ismail's home was a sanctuary of love and laughter, where warmth embraced anyone who crossed the threshold. As per tradition, his children dashed to welcome 'Aunt Jeannie' at the door, their faces radiant with anticipation. And Jeannie, never one to disappoint, had brought along thoughtful gifts for each child, tailored to their individual tastes and interests.

"What about me?" Ismail queried playfully as he and his wife emerged from the bustling kitchen. His wife hit him on the shoulder.

"I'm sorry, Jeannie. My husband is such a big baby."

Jeannie chuckled and playfully teased, "Oh, you don't have to remind me. Hey, buddy, this is for you and the entire family."

His curiosity piqued, Ismail examined the large manila folder in his hands. "What is it?" he inquired with a grin.

With a mischievous twinkle in her eye, Jeannie responded, "I thought you said you were a highly-trained FBI agent. May I suggest you open it to find out?" Laughter filled the room as Ismail eagerly tore open the envelope.

As the picture of Jeannie's majestic beachfront mansion in Myrtle Beach emerged, Ismail's face lit up with amazement. "Whose house is this?" he wondered aloud, captivated by the breathtaking view of the ocean visible through the glass front door.

"Look, Ace," Jeannie exclaimed, "you're long overdue for a vacation. These plane tickets to and from Myrtle Beach are your escape. My house is right on the beach."

Overwhelmed with gratitude, Ismail could hardly contain his excitement. Jeannie continued, "Once you arrive, arrange for an Uber or a cab to take you to the house. It's conveniently close to the Myrtle Beach International Airport."

Ismail's wife chimed in, suggesting, "Wouldn't it be better to rent a car at the airport?"

Jeannie shook her head with a knowing smile. "No need. I have a car at the house, waiting for you to use."

The children eagerly examined a picture of a sleek new Porsche shown parked at the house, each one vying for the first chance to drive it. Laughter filled the room as they discussed who would get behind the wheel.

Ismail then pulled brochures from the envelope, feigning bewilderment. Jeannie playfully teased, "You're not such a great investigator after all."

With amusement, Jeannie clarified, "Inside, you'll find tickets for the Pirate Voyage Dinner/Show, the Alligator Experience, Ripley's Hollywood wax museum and Aquarium, a Dolphin Cruise, and the largest water park in South Carolina. I've also arranged for you and the kids to enjoy a range of watersports, from parasailing to kayaking, jet skis, and even a thrilling banana boat ride. Just give me a call when you're ready to go, and I'll make all the arrangements."

The younger kids, bubbling with excitement, began bouncing with anticipation, eager to embark on their adventures. Ismail's wife was moved to tears, her joy overflowing. Ismail, touched by Jeannie's generosity, could only mouth a heartfelt "thank you" as he gazed at his dear friend, knowing that this extraordinary gift would create cherished memories for his family.

"Let it be known that, here and now, in the presence of your entire family, I am issuing a directive. You have seven days to submit your vacation date preferences to me so I can facilitate the necessary arrangements. Consider it a mandate."

"Yes, boss lady. I'll handle that during our breakfast tomorrow, and you can expect it on your desk bright and early Monday morning." He sparked another round of laughter from the group with a cheerful salute to Jeannie.

La Pergo Restaurant, perched on a hill, offered an enchanting view of the Eternal City, its beauty unrivaled as the Italian sun bathed the landscape in its warm glow. However, the breathtaking vista held little significance for the three cardinals who occupied a discreet backroom, concealed from the gaze of the restaurant's guests. Their choice of location was strategic, as La Pergo was renowned as one of the finest dining establishments in all of Rome. By 4 p.m. it would be teeming with patrons, but at this moment, their privacy remained assured.

Cardinal Rodger McCormick was seated with a direct view of the restaurant's main dining room. To his left sat Cardinal Agostino Vallini, and to his right, Cardinal Francis Mahoney. All three men were in their early seventies and bore the weight of their years with grace. Each had a glass of red wine before them, occasionally bringing it to their lips for a sip.

Cardinal Vallini broke the silence in hushed tones, his words weighed down with significance. "I received a communication early this morning, informing me that the Sodarium is now in our possession," he whispered to the other two. "The party expects payment within one week. Cardinal Mahoney, I believe it falls upon you to transport the funds to Spain."

Cardinal Mahoney nodded, his resolve evident. "That will not be an issue," he affirmed. "However, have we determined the appropriate location to house the relic once the transaction is complete and I have taken possession of it?" He directed his question to the two cardinals beside him, seeking their guidance.

Cardinal McCormick met Mahoney's gaze and his response was measured, "Indeed, we have a plan in place. You will convey the Sodarium to Father Paul at the Church of Santa Maria de le Corte. He is prepared to receive you and has a secure facility ready to ensure the relic's meticulous care."

Cardinal Mahoney, while committed to the mission, couldn't help but express his apprehension. "Do you believe it is wise to place the sacred relic so close to the very place from which it was stolen?" he questioned, a touch of nervousness tainting his voice.

Cardinal Vallini leaned in, a sly smile crossing his face as he offered his rationale. "What better place than right under the vigilant eyes of the Italian police and the Vatican security force? It's the last location they would suspect. Let them guard the vaults and archives while we maintain our grip on the prize." He raised his wine class, "To the new Catholic Church."

The three cardinals paused, sharing a moment of contemplation as they raised their glasses in unison and toasted their audacious plan. In that private enclave, with the beauty of Rome unfolding beyond the window, they embarked on a journey that would test their cunning and conviction, with the Sodarium as the coveted jewel at the heart of their clandestine endeavor.

CHAPTER FIVE

The next Monday morning, Jeannie was tired after wrestling with another particularly challenging night of restless sleep, courtesy of her relentless headache. As she tuned in to Newsmax hoping to catch updates on the Sodarium theft, her disappointment was palpable as the topic remained conspicuously absent. Struggling to find her appetite, she attempted to nibble on an English muffin but quickly felt a wave of nausea, opting instead for a soothing cup of milk.

Persistent bouts of vertigo and lightheadedness served as unwelcome companions. Nevertheless, she mustered her determination and readied herself for the commute across the Dumbarton Bridge to the FBI office in San Francisco. Her rationale was simple: immersing herself in the workload might just be the remedy needed to chase the headache away. She did, however, remember to make a quick call to her doctor as soon as she arrived, knowing that her well-being was a priority.

Jeannie was an early bird as she made her way to the breakroom, appreciating the solitude in the quiet office. She prepared a comforting cup of herbal tea, the steam wafting upward and mingling with the first glimpse of daylight. Her boss, Special Agent in Charge (SAC) Lomax, appeared shortly after, pouring himself a coffee and adding powdered creamer and sugar.

"Good morning," Lomax greeted her. "How was your weekend?" he inquired, leaning against the counter with a touch of concern in his eyes.

"Uneventful," Jeannie responded with a faint smile. " I was nursing a terrible headache most of the time. I plan to call my doctor at eight to see if I can secure an appointment with her."

Lomax nodded in understanding, "My wife experiences migraines occasionally," he shared. "She mentions seeing spots in her vision when she closes her eyes, and over-the-counter drugs don't provide much relief. Her doctor prescribed some medication to take when she feels a migraine coming on. Perhaps your doctor will offer a similar solution."

Jeannie sighed in relief, sharing her experience, "Hell, I hope so. I was up for most of the night. I'm hoping that once I immerse myself in my work, the headache will dissipate on its own."

Lomax leaned in with a concerned expression, "Well, if it doesn't improve, I want you to take it easy and leave the office. There's nothing here that's so urgent we can't manage without you."

Jeannie appreciated Lomax's understanding and concern for her well-being, reinforcing the camaraderie that existed among her colleagues. As she sipped her tea, she felt reassured by the support of her team, knowing they would look out for her if needed.

Cardinal Mahoney touched down at Asturias airport, where a luxurious stretch limousine stood ready to whisk him away, his belongings secured and taken care of. The journey to the grand fortress of Vincent D'Amico, which stretched over the medieval landscape, was undertaken in silence, with the Cardinal in awe of the immense effort and craftsmanship that had clearly gone into constructing this ancient masterpiece from the Middle Ages.

All three Cardinals had fervently hoped that the theft of the Sodarium could be executed without a drop of blood being spilled, a silent prayer for peace echoing within them. The relic was undeniably precious, but the mission to safeguard and reinforce the bedrock of traditional Catholic doctrine was an even weightier burden on his shoulders. It was a duty that transcended the bounds of time, and one that connected him to centuries of faithful believers who had gone before him.

Meeting with Vincent D'Amico marked a pivotal moment in Mahoney's life. He had only heard cautionary whispers from Cardinal Vallini about the ruthlessness of the thief and his enigmatic henchmen. They had learned that the Sodarium's theft had resulted in the tragic death of a priest, an event that cast a shadow over their mission. It was a stark reminder that preserving their faith and battling against the progressive movement championed by Pope Francis had consequences more profound than they initially comprehended.

As he stepped into the castle, he was welcomed by a remarkably athletic woman, later revealed as Natalia, one of Vincent D'Amico's most reliable bodyguards. Her striking, raven-colored hair cascaded down her back, framing her arresting green eyes, and her captivating presence was so commanding that she could have effortlessly graced the catwalks of any nation she chose to represent.

"Please, follow me," were the sole words that Natalia uttered, prompting Cardinal Mahoney to trail behind her bearing a substantial suitcase containing the agreed payment for D'Amico in exchange for the revered Sudarium. Their route through the imposing castle was deliberate, finally revealing a grand room with towering twelve-foot-tall walls adorned with an impressive collection of mostly first-edition books reaching from floor to ceiling. The marble floor underfoot rivaled the splendor of the Vatican itself.

On the fourth wall, also stretching from floor to ceiling, an enormous aquarium took center stage housing hundreds of colorful fish, with a shark or graceful ray occasionally swimming past. Before this aquatic spectacle, a majestic 14-foot mahogany desk commanded attention, adorned with intricate carvings and a glass inlay housing numerous quartz crystals in shades of purple, green, red, and blue. The warm glow of the desk lamp cast enchanting, almost ethereal, radiance upon the quartz beneath the protective glass.

Vincent D'Amico exuded an air of authority as he sat behind this piece of furniture. Clad in an impeccably tailored designer suit and tie, he scrutinized Cardinal Mahoney with keen eyes before gesturing for him to take a seat in an ornate chair placed across from him.

"Thank you, Natalia," D'Amico acknowledged with a nod, and upon his cue, Natalia gracefully exited the room, her presence fading into the distance. With a glance toward the formidable mahogany desk that separated them, D'Amico turned his attention back to Cardinal Mahoney.

"Yes, indeed," Mahoney replied, shifting slightly as he prepared to hand over the suitcase. "I have brought the agreed-upon sum for the relic. Would you like me to place it on your desk for inspection?"

D'Amico leaned back in his ornate leather chair, his expression a mixture of authority and underlying caution. "No need for that, Cardinal Mahoney. A man of your stature and standing within the Church wouldn't risk tainting your reputation. Imagine the scandal it would cause if it ever came to light that you and your fellow Cardinals orchestrated the Sudarium's theft." The unspoken threat was a weighty reminder of the stakes involved.

An imposing, muscle-bound figure entered the room and promptly picked up the suitcase, disappearing with it as silently as he had arrived. The silence endured in the dim, mesmerizing glow of the quartz crystals on the mahogany desk and the light from the aquarium.

"Now, before we proceed to the Sudarium, I believe you and your fellow Cardinals have the authority to negotiate the next holy relic's retrieval, correct?" D'Amico inquired, his gaze penetrating.

Cardinal Mahoney cleared his throat, choosing his words carefully. "Yes, we have reached an agreement regarding your price for acquiring the next sacred artifact. Do you have an approximate timeline for its retrieval?"

A sardonic smile curved D'Amico's lips as he replied, "The endeavor requires meticulous planning that takes time, but rest assured, you shall have the article before Easter. A fitting timeline, wouldn't you say?" His words held a chilling edge as he contemplated the implications of their unholy partnership.

"Now, let us lay our eyes upon the cherished cloth that you and your fellow conspirators covet so dearly,"

D'Amico suggested, his tone laced with a curious mixture of intrigue and authority. Cardinal Mahoney obediently followed him, descending a long spiral staircase that bore a striking resemblance to the way to the dank dungeons of the Middle Ages, where the unfortunate met their inescapable fate at the hands of merciless torturers.

D'Amico paused briefly to explain their choice of location. "I selected this underground chamber precisely for its utility. It allows me to maintain precise control over the humidity and environmental conditions required to safeguard the relic. It's already been placed within a suitable container, designed to preserve the specific conditions until you can secure it at a more permanent location."

As they ventured further into the depths of the underground chamber, Cardinal Mahoney couldn't help but contemplate the significance of their unholy alliance, the secrecy, and the lengths they were willing to go to safeguard the traditional Catholic doctrine, all within the chilling ambiance of this subterranean sanctuary.

Upon their arrival in the dungeon, Cardinal Mahoney's eyes fell upon the Sudarium that was prominently displayed in the center of the room. A solitary chair was positioned in front of the ancient cloth where a single person could sit and contemplate the sacred relic.

D'Amico gestured toward the chair, his voice tinged with a hint of indifference, "I've taken the liberty of sitting here several times since coming into possession of the Sudarium, and honestly, I fail to see what all the fuss is about.

"To my eyes, it appears to be nothing more than a piece of deteriorating fabric, adorned with what could be bloodstains but might as well be fading red paint. Yet, if the faithful continue to place their unwavering trust in it and are willing to compensate me generously for the retrieval of the next relic, then, by all means, be my guest."

The muscular man reappeared, prompting D'Amico's approval with a nod. He carefully took hold of the container safeguarding the Sudarium and motioned for Cardinal Mahoney to follow. No parting words or acknowledgments were offered by D'Amico as they departed. It was only when Cardinal Mahoney had ascended halfway up the spiraling staircase that he realized D'Amico had vanished, leaving behind a lingering sense of enigma and uncertainty.

CHAPTER SIX

Jeannie considered herself fortunate when an unexpected cancellation allowed her to meet with her doctor on Monday afternoon. She had dutifully informed Special Agent in Charge Lomax that she would be stepping out temporarily and had placed Ismail in charge during her absence. After a final check-in with her secretary, she made her way toward the exit leading to the secure parking lot.

As she reached for the door, a familiar voice chimed in from behind her. "Hey, boss lady. I hope the doctor can work some magic and get you some relief from that pesky headache," Ismail remarked, his concern evident in his tone.

"Thanks, buddy," Jeannie replied with a grateful smile. "If you need to reach me for anything while I'm out, don't hesitate to call."

Ismail couldn't help but tease her, his eyes twinkling mischievously. "Well, if you decide to take a couple of weeks off, I can start moving my things back into your office." His broad grin conveyed the playful banter he was known for.

Jeannie couldn't help but chuckle, shaking her head at his audacious suggestion. "Not going to happen, Ace. Besides, you and the family have that getaway to Myrtle Beach coming up in a few weeks. Don't forget, or your wife might just skin you alive." With a friendly wave, she turned and headed toward her appointment, leaving her trusted colleague with a smile on his face and a reminder of his impending family obligations.

Dr. Pam Shelby had been practicing medicine for as long as Jeannie had been an FBI agent. Their mutual respect for each other's professions was evident in their interactions. Dr. Shelby often confided that she could never handle the relentless stress that Jeannie faced daily. The two women were the same age, making it easy for Jeannie to confide in her long-time friend about her health concerns.

Entering the examination room after a polite knock, Dr. Shelby greeted Jeannie warmly. "Hello, Jeannie. How's my favorite secret agent doing today?"

Jeannie offered a genuine smile. "Hello, Pam. It's always nice to see you. I've been dealing with some rather bothersome headaches that come and go. I tried over-the-counter meds, but they only provide minimal relief."

Dr. Shelby began her examination, gently feeling around Jeannie's scalp. "Have you had any recent head injuries or bumps?" she inquired.

Jeannie furrowed her brow in thought. "No, not that I can recall."

"Well, your blood pressure is slightly elevated, but it's still within the normal range, so I can rule out hypertension. Have you been more stressed than usual?" Dr. Shelby inquired.

Jeannie shook her head. "No, actually, my workload has been relatively low. It's almost as if it's the calm before the storm."

Dr. Shelby considered this information. "Hmm. You're probably already aware, but migraines can cause severe throbbing pain or a pulsing sensation, usually concentrated on one side of the head. They often come with symptoms like nausea, vomiting, and extreme sensitivity to light and sound. Migraine attacks can last for hours to days, and the pain can be so intense that it interferes with your daily activities. Have you been experiencing any of these symptoms?"

Jeannie nodded, acknowledging the symptoms she had been experiencing. "Yes, and sometimes I feel lightheaded with a touch of vertigo."

Dr. Shelby continued her inquiry, seeking a comprehensive medical history. "Has anyone in your family ever had migraines?"

Jeannie took a moment to reflect on the question. "My stepmom did experience bouts of vertigo and the occasional headache, but I don't recall her describing them as migraines."

Dr. Shelby's next question shifted to Jeannie's biological family. "What about your biological mom?"

Jeannie's expression softened with a hint of sadness. "Well, as I've told you before, I never had the chance to meet or get to know my mom. In fact, I didn't even discover her existence until after her passing."

"Understood," Dr. Shelby said empathetically. "For now, I'm going to prescribe a mild dose of Migranal, a nasal spray that is most effective when taken shortly after the onset of migraine symptoms. It tends to provide relief for a little longer than 24 hours. While it's rare, it's worth noting that there can be some side effects, such as potential worsening of migraine-related vomiting and nausea."

She continued, "Additionally, I'll prescribe Maxalt-MLT pills, which work to block pain pathways in the brain. Take these twice a day. I'd like to see you again in two weeks to assess your progress and make any necessary adjustments to your treatment." Dr. Shelby's words were reassuring, instilling a sense of trust and confidence in her patient.

After her doctor's appointment, Jeannie decided to wrap up her day and get a head start on her commute to Fremont. She planned to swing by her pharmacist, expecting that her prescriptions would be ready by the time she arrived since she was starting to feel the onset of a headache. She thought, "Might as well grab some dinner on the way back because I really don't feel like cooking tonight."

During the appointment, her doctor had given her some crucial advice to start keeping a record of her migraine attacks. "Note the time of day they occur, document what you were doing when they started, and keep track of how long they last. The medication I prescribed should be effective, but if, over the next two weeks, your symptoms persist or worsen, please don't hesitate to call me, and I'll arrange an appointment with a neurologist for you, okay?"

Jeannie was committed to following her doctor's advice diligently. She knew that monitoring her symptoms and medication's effectiveness was essential in managing her migraines. As she headed to the pharmacy, she contemplated how this record-keeping might help her regain control over her life and get relief from these debilitating headaches.

Vincent D'Amico convened his loyal crew within the opulent confines of his castle office. Earlier, he had taken the initiative to arrange seats for all the attendees, ensuring that the meeting space was comfortable and conducive to their upcoming discussion. As his crew members gathered, he skillfully lowered a screen from the ceiling and connected his laptop, an act that signaled the beginning of an important briefing.

"Alright, gang," Vincent began, his commanding presence resonating in the room, "Let's begin. This is our next target." With a deft click of a button, he advanced the slide, causing a compelling image to materialize on the large screen before them. The image was none other than the revered Shroud of Turin, the fabled burial cloth that had purportedly enveloped Jesus Christ's body after his crucifixion. It had been safeguarded within the hallowed confines of the Cathedral of St. John the Baptist in Turin, Italy, for over four centuries.

Vincent allowed a moment for his crew to absorb the significance of their new mission. The room was filled with reverence and anticipation, knowing they were embarking on a venture that held immense historical and spiritual weight.

Vincent continued, his voice tinged with respect for their target, "We must acknowledge that the security surrounding this relic is, without a doubt, as sophisticated, if not more so, than that of the Sudarium." The crew members exchanged knowing glances, fully aware of the daunting challenges they were about to face. Vincent D'Amico's eyes met theirs, conveying the gravity of the task ahead and the determination needed to accomplish their mission.

He retrieved a series of sealed envelopes from a discreet desk drawer, each bearing the name of an individual in the room, as he addressed his assembled team. "Ladies and gentlemen, as we've done in the past, these packets contain your respective missions," he explained, distributing the envelopes. "Each one of you, except Natalia, has a window of ten days to meticulously devise and finalize your plan."

Vincent turned his gaze toward Natalia, who had a unique role within the group. "Natalia," he began, his tone warm and confident, "as in our previous endeavors, your charm and finesse will be key to gaining invaluable insights that are otherwise unattainable. You've been granted a more generous timeframe of 21 days to work your magic and secure the information we need."

The mention of their ambitious target didn't escape the team's notice. Vincent emphasized, "The value of this theft far exceeds that of the Sudarium, but it's imperative to note that, following our last operation's resounding success, the Catholic Church is likely to have bolstered its security measures considerably. This challenge won't be a walk in the park."

With the distribution of tasks and timelines clarified, Vincent encouraged his team to begin their preparations. "Now, go and get started," he urged them. As the members of the group started to leave, one by one making their way toward the door, Vincent suddenly halted their exit. "Natalia," he called, his voice holding a hint of intrigue. The final person to leave obediently closed the door behind them, leaving the two of them alone in the vast, dimly lit room.

Natalia's eyes, filled with a potent mixture of desire and determination, remained locked on Vincent's. She slowly and sensually traced her steps around the massive desk, her nimble fingers undoing the buttons of her sapphire blouse. Each undone button exposed a bit more of her ebony bra, accentuating her ample chest as she moved with a tantalizing grace, alluding to the depths of her talents beyond the apparent allure.

CHAPTER SEVEN

VATICAN

In a spacious and solemn chamber, nine cardinals occupied imposing chairs, flanked by a group of eight trusted advisors and a diligent secretary. Their collective presence filled the room with an air of anticipation, awaiting the arrival of none other than Pope Francis himself.

This assembly, known as the Council of Cardinals, was informally referred to as the "C9" due to its consistent composition of nine cardinal members. Pope Francis had carefully handpicked these cardinals, a group of unwavering supporters, with the sole purpose of guiding him in the comprehensive reform of the Catholic Church. The council's inception was officially marked on September 28, 2013, and it represented a pivotal step in the Pope's mission to address and resolve the intricate issues and challenges facing the Church.

As these esteemed members gathered within the hallowed chamber, they shared not only their individual wisdom and insights but also a profound commitment to Pope Francis's vision for a revitalized and progressive Catholic Church. Their roles were instrumental in shaping the future of the faith, and their presence symbolized the unity and dedication of those at the heart of this transformative journey.

A profound hush fell over the assembled group at the entrance of Pope Francis. Each member rose from their seats, standing in solemn reverence, and they continued to maintain their respectful silence even after the Pontiff had settled into his chair. Pope Francis, with a humble nod of acknowledgment, gestured for them to retake their seats.

Amid this atmosphere of respectful contemplation, the Pope began to address the council. His voice, carrying the weight of his spiritual authority and concern, resonated through the room. "As all of you are undoubtedly aware," he began, "several days ago, audacious transgressors infiltrated the sacred confines of the temple that safeguarded the revered Sudarium. Our security forces have been collaborating closely with Spanish law enforcement authorities in the wake of this grievous incident. Yet, regrettably, despite their tireless efforts, as of today, the ongoing investigation has not yielded any significant insights into the identity of those who orchestrated this brazen theft."

Everyone present could feel the seriousness of the crisis as Pope Francis shared this disheartening update with his trusted council. The Sudarium's theft was a wound to the heart of the Church, and the Pontiff's words served as a solemn reminder of the challenges that lay ahead in restoring its sanctity and addressing the actions of the unknown culprits.

Cardinal Rodriguez, a respected and thoughtful member of the council, raised a tentative hand, seeking Pope Francis's permission to speak. The Pontiff acknowledged him with a gentle nod and welcoming gesture.

Cardinal Rodriguez cleared his throat and began, "Your Holiness, might it be possible that those responsible for the theft were motivated by opposition to the transformative reforms you've been tirelessly championing within the Church? There are traditionalists among us who fervently resist those changes and may see the Sudarium as a symbol of the Church's sacred traditions. They might view its theft as an act of defiance, an attempt to undermine your progressive agenda."

Pope Francis considered the cardinal's words thoughtfully, recognizing the complex interplay of ideologies within the Church. He acknowledged, "Your observation is astute, Cardinal Rodriguez. The resistance to our reforms has been palpable, and some individuals may, indeed, resort to desperate measures to oppose them. However, let us not forget the more pragmatic possibility. The prospect of financial gain, the allure of a substantial reward from the Church or other interested parties, could be a powerful incentive for those with less noble intentions."

The council members listened intently, knowing this was a pivotal moment in their quest to uncover the truth behind the Sudarium's theft. The conversation now encompassed the delicate balance between the ideological opposition to reform and the allure of material gain, leaving them with a perplexing challenge to unravel.

Jeannie strolled into the office a bit later than her usual time, a faint crease of discomfort etched on her face. The persistent headache that had plagued her throughout the night showed no signs of relenting, though she optimistically attributed it to the new medication taking its time to kick in.

Ismail, with his characteristic grin, playfully teased her as he held a steaming cup of coffee and a tempting donut. "About time you showed up. Now I have to cancel the moving crew who were all set to deliver my hot tub to your office."

Jeannie's eyes twinkled with a mischievous glint as she retorted, "Well, Ismail, you better watch out! All those donuts and hot tub sessions might add a few inches to your waistline, and that handsome

Portuguese physique you keep bragging about could go to pot."

His teasing banter continued as Jeannie leaned on the corner of her desk. "No offense, boss, but you look tired as hell. Did you get any sleep last night? I did tell you to send the guy home early so you could catch some much-needed rest."

Jeannie sighed with a wry smile, appreciative of Ismail's concern. "Oh, it's quite heartwarming to have someone looking out for me. As a matter of fact, I had another headache throughout the night. Unfortunately, it's still too early for the meds I got from my doctor yesterday to take effect. Thank you very much for caring, Ismail, now get to work."

She headed for the break room, but the odor of coffee seemed to make her more nauseous. She made a quick exit and went to the lady's room. There, the urge to vomit continued for a few minutes before the spell passed. She washed her face with cold water, felt a little better, and once again, tried to make it to her office. She felt lightheaded and that she was losing her balance, so she braced herself on her secretary's desk.

"Are you okay?" Ismail asked who was coming up behind her to continue his banter. He placed his hand on her shoulder, and she grabbed it to steady herself.

"Yeah, thanks. It's that damn headache."

"What's happening?" a concerned-looking Lomax asked as he was making his way to the break room for a third cup of coffee.

"Jeannie's having a little dizzy spell," Ismail explained, his voice tinged with concern. "Her doctor prescribed some medication, but it hasn't kicked in yet."

Jeannie, her hand resting lightly on her temple, responded with a reassuring tone, "I'll be okay; I just need to sit down in my office."

Lomax, her superior, interjected firmly, "No, you're not, young lady. Ismail, take Jeannie home. Find Darcy and have her follow you in Jeannie's car. Jeannie, I want you to take the rest of the week off. Those are my orders. Ismail, go find Darcy. I'll stay here with Jeannie."

Jeannie couldn't help but feel a bit embarrassed by the situation and said so to Lomax and her secretary.

Lomax, who understood the toll of migraines, offered reassurance. "Nonsense. When my wife gets hit with a migraine, it takes hours, sometimes days, to bounce back. Go home, lay on the couch with a cold compress, and follow the doctor's orders."

Ismail soon returned with a concerned Darcy in tow. She approached Jeannie with a worried expression. "Jeannie, are you okay?" Darcy inquired, her concern palpable.

With a faint smile, Jeannie reassured them, "Just a darn headache. Lomax says I need to go home."

Ismail, ever the joker, couldn't resist adding some levity to the situation. "There's nothing to be sorry about, especially since I will have to drive your car."

Darcy, always ready to join in the fun, teased Ismail in response, "Hey, why can't I drive the Ferrari?" The exchange brought a moment of light-heartedness despite Jeannie's discomfort.

CHAPTER EIGHT

A brisk knock on the director's door preceded Sean Delaney's entrance into his office, the clock ticking down with just two minutes to spare.

"Good morning, Delaney," the director greeted him with a nod.

"Good morning, Sir," Delaney replied respectfully as he took a seat, settling into the chair across from his superior.

The director wasted no time in commending Delaney for his recent operation. "Your handling of the Chinese bioweapons specialist was nothing short of impressive. The explosion you orchestrated at his research facility was a stroke of brilliance. You not only eliminated the target, but you also wiped out the biohazard materials and all of his research."

Delaney offered a humble nod in response. "Thank you, Sir."

An uneasy silence enveloped the room, with both men aware of the unspoken truth that lingered in the air. What had just been discussed was now firmly in the past, a completed chapter in Delaney's clandestine career. The enigmatic organization he now served, in stark contrast to his previous tenure with Interpol, was poised for new and even more covert missions. An intricate web of secrecy and intrigue was about to unfurl its threads once again, and Sean Delaney, the elusive operative, was ready to embrace his new role with determination and purpose.

"Are you a religious man, Delaney?" The unexpected question sent a subtle ripple of discomfort through Sean Delaney, making him shift slightly in his chair as he grappled with his response.

"I believe in God," he began, carefully choosing his words, "but I'm not affiliated with any particular church or denomination. May I ask why you're inquiring?" Delaney's curiosity about the intent behind the question was evident in his earnest gaze. However, his supervisor didn't offer an immediate response, opting to scrutinize Delaney as if searching for something deeper.

The director's next question took a sharp turn into uncharted territory, prompting Delaney to delve into the realm of historical and religious intrigue. "What do you know about the Sudarium, the relic that was said to have covered Jesus after he was taken down from the cross?"

Delaney's eyebrows furrowed as he contemplated the unexpected turn in the conversation. The Sudarium was not a topic that typically arose in his line of work. "The Sudarium of Oviedo," he mused, "the cloth that supposedly covered the face of Jesus when he was taken down from the cross. I've heard it mentioned in historical and religious contexts."

His supervisor nodded, his expression maintaining an air of profound interest. "Indeed, the Sudarium is often referred to as the face cloth of Christ. Some claim it bears his image, imprinted during that fateful moment of his passion and crucifixion.

Delaney's interest deepened. "I've heard the cloth has been the subject of extensive research and debate, both from scientific and religious perspectives. Some consider it an important relic with significant historical and spiritual significance."

The director leaned forward, revealing a hint of a secretive smile. "It has, and this cloth holds a special place in the mission you're about to undertake, Delaney. Your unique background and perspective might prove invaluable. You're being tasked with a mission that combines history, faith, and secrecy."

With this revelation, Delaney understood that his journey into the enigmatic world of intelligence and espionage was about to intersect with a realm of history and spirituality that he could never have anticipated.

The Sudarium, a symbol of both faith and intrigue, was now entwined with his next mission, promising to unveil a new layer of challenges and mysteries.

"Several days ago," the director continued, "a shocking incident occurred. The Sudarium was stolen from its revered location in Spain."

Delaney nodded, his knowledge of the situation clear. "The Cathedral of San Salvador, in Oviedo, Spain," he affirmed.

The director's brows furrowed, momentarily taken aback. "What?" he exclaimed, his surprise evident in his tone.

"That's the place where the Sudarium was safeguarded, to the best of my recollection," Delaney replied, exuding a subtle air of confidence in his knowledge.

After a moment of gathering his thoughts, the director acknowledged Delaney's information. "Oh, yes," he finally responded, as if realizing the connection, "the cathedral in Spain, indeed."

The stolen Sudarium's significance was now even more apparent, with Delaney's familiarity with its whereabouts lending his involvement in the upcoming mission an added layer of intrigue and depth. As the director and Delaney delved deeper into the unfolding situation, it became clear that the stolen relic held not only historical and spiritual importance but also the key to an enigma that would challenge their skills and instincts in unforeseen ways.

"When the Sudarium was first taken, the National Police Agency in Spain undertook a discreet investigation, striving to maintain an air of confidentiality. However, as the gravity of the situation unfolded, a dramatic shift occurred. The Vatican's formidable security force, renowned for its unyielding commitment to safeguarding religious artifacts and historical relics, asserted jurisdiction over the case.

"In a somewhat unexpected turn of events, the Vatican's security force then reached out to your former agency, Interpol, to extend an invitation for their collaborative expertise. The prospect of this union was grounded in a calculated hope – the belief that the audacious culprits behind the Sudarium's theft might ultimately aim to sell this sacred relic to the highest bidder."

Delaney processed what the director had just dropped on his lap. This collaboration between the Vatican and Interpol signaled a potent fusion of secular and spiritual realms, an alliance where the preservation of faith, history, and security converged in pursuit of a common goal. It was a mission that transcended mere law enforcement, encompassing a realm of cultural heritage and reverence that few could fathom.

Curiosity and determination were etched into Delaney's expression as he considered the complexity of the task before him. "I assume they haven't identified any suspects or received any ransom demands at this point?" he inquired, already formulating a mental blueprint for his initial moves.

The director nodded in affirmation. "You're correct on both counts. Your flight to Spain is scheduled for three hours. Good luck, Delaney," he said, signaling the end of their meeting.

With a succinct dismissal, Delaney rose from his chair and exited the director's office. There were no formal parting words exchanged, but the unspoken understanding of the gravity of the mission hung in the air, setting the stage for an adventure that would demand every ounce of his expertise and ingenuity.

CHAPTER NINE

After three days had elapsed, Jeannie's persistent headaches, though slightly less frequent, remained stubbornly intense. Frustrated and eager to find a solution, she took it upon herself to reach out to her doctor's office, a decision that would unveil unexpected developments. To her surprise, it was none other than Dr. Shelby, her physician, who promptly returned her call.

As her cell phone displayed Dr. Shelby's name on the caller ID, Jeannie answered with a sense of anticipation. "Hello, Dr. Shelby," she greeted the doctor.

"Hello, Jeannie," Dr. Shelby's voice held genuine concern. "I'm sorry to hear that the medication I prescribed hasn't been as effective as we'd hoped. Considering your condition, I've pulled a few strings.

If you're available, I've arranged for you to see Dr. Goldsmith, an outstanding neurologist, tomorrow morning at 9 a.m. However, before your appointment with him, there's an MRI scheduled at 2:15 today in Fremont. Can you make it?"

Jeannie agreed to the MRI, understanding the importance of taking every possible step to pinpoint the cause of her distress. Normally, an MRI was a routine medical procedure for her, but this time, it proved to be far from easy. As she lay inside the machine, the mechanical hum and claustrophobic confines triggered an unexpected wave of nausea. It was a grueling experience, and she fought hard to endure it.

When the MRI concluded, Jeannie staggered out, her pale face reflecting the toll the procedure had taken on her. She rushed to the nearest restroom and, with a sinking feeling, emptied the contents of her stomach, the culmination of a small lunch that was now wasted. The unanticipated hardship of the MRI served as a stark reminder that her journey toward finding relief and answers was no simple task, and the road ahead would demand both patience and resilience. Now, she had to wait until the following morning when she would hopefully learn from Dr. Goldsmith what was causing her affliction.

With his fellow conspirators present, Vincent D'Amico once again lowered a screen from the ceiling in his castle office. He turned down the lights on his desk and the ones illuminating his giant aquarium. Once the screen descended, he began by displaying the Shroud of Turin.

"For those who may not be familiar with it, allow me to introduce the Shroud of Turin. This enigmatic artifact, also referred to as the Holy Shroud, is a piece of linen cloth that holds a faint but haunting image within its fibers, depicting a man's front and back. This mysterious relic has garnered reverence and intrigue for centuries, finding its most fervent devotees among members of the Catholic Church.

"According to tradition, the Shroud is believed to be the very burial cloth that was employed to enshroud the body of Jesus of Nazareth immediately following his crucifixion. What sets this cloth apart and fuels its veneration is the miraculous image that seemingly materialized upon it, bearing the likeness of Jesus himself.

"This ancient and revered artifact, which resides in Turin, Italy, has been the subject of intense scrutiny, debate, and wonder. It has piqued the curiosity of the faithful and the inquisitive alike as they seek to unravel the mysteries surrounding its origins, its authenticity, and the nature of the image it bears."

Vincent paused, giving everyone in the room a moment to digest his weighty words. "Now, as for all the intricacies and ethical dilemmas surrounding this matter," he continued, "they need not trouble us as long as there are generous benefactors willing to open their wallets wide for the privilege of ownership." His statement elicited a collective chuckle from the audience.

In that brief moment of mirth, the room seemed to momentarily set aside the complexities and moral quandaries that often accompany such discussions. It was as if they had collectively chosen to embrace the practical, business-oriented perspective that Vincent had just put forth. After all, in the world of commerce, it's not uncommon for financial incentives to trump concerns of a more philosophical or ethical nature.

This casual reaction hinted at the overarching pragmatism of the group. They understood that decisions were frequently driven by profit margins and market dynamics rather than ethical considerations in the realm of financial dealings. And for now, at least, they were content to share a hearty laugh at the prospect of big financial gains, putting aside the deeper questions for another time.

He moved forward to the next slide, unveiling crucial details. "Let me paint the picture for you," he began, his voice measured and deliberate. "The Shroud of Turin is no ordinary artifact. It's a fragile treasure, meticulously safeguarded in a highly secure environment. This irreplaceable relic resides beneath layers of laminated bulletproof glass encased in an airtight chamber.

"The conditions within this chamber are precisely controlled, maintaining a consistent temperature and humidity. The atmosphere is composed of argon (99.5%) and oxygen (0.5%) to prevent chemical changes. This may sound like an overly cautious approach, but it's essential to preserving the cloth's integrity."

He went on to emphasize the logistical intricacies of their audacious plan. "Once we acquire the Shroud, we must meticulously replicate and maintain this controlled environment until we receive our payment. The Shroud rests on an aluminum support that can slide on runners, and it's stored flat within a secure case."

He then elaborated on the security measures protecting the Shroud. "Understand that security for the Shroud of Turin is exceedingly tight. It is rarely unveiled to the public eye, and when it is, it's under the vigilant watch of security cameras and more layers of bulletproof glass.

"A significant security challenge arose in 1997 when a fire broke out in the Cathedral of Saint John the Baptist. Firefighters had to breach four layers of bulletproof glass to protect the Shroud, underscoring the lengths taken to safeguard it."

He paused momentarily to stress the Shroud's unique fragility. "Due to its extremely delicate state, it remains hidden from public view except during very infrequent public exhibitions. The most recent of these exhibitions occurred in 2015 and drew millions of visitors. Regrettably, there are currently no plans for another public display in the near future."

He then shifted the focus to their key asset. "This is why we are heavily reliant on Natalia's insider access to gain more critical information before we can proceed. I wanted to provide you all with this update to make it clear just what challenges we face on this mission. Alright, let's get back to work."

The room was left with a deeper understanding of the intricacies and vulnerabilities surrounding their ambitious undertaking, reinforcing the importance of Natalia's role in navigating these treacherous waters.

CHAPTER TEN

Delaney's arrival in Oviedo was marked by a seamless transition as he checked into the luxurious Hotel de la Reconquista, strategically located in the heart of the city. This elegant establishment occupies a stunning 18th-century building that has earned the distinguished status of being declared a national monument. The hotel's architecture exudes a captivating baroque style, an embodiment of historical grandeur that immediately transports guests to a bygone era.

While the Hotel de la Reconquista has retained its classical charm, it has seamlessly integrated modern comforts into its offerings. In this regard, it stood shoulder-to-shoulder with the other prestigious five-star hotels Delaney frequently patronized. Each air-conditioned room, designed for ultimate comfort, features contemporary amenities that cater to the needs of discerning guests. A flat-screen TV provides entertainment, a well-stocked mini-bar is at one's disposal, and a spacious work desk ensures convenience for those with business matters to address. In addition, a secure safe is available for the safekeeping of valuable possessions.

The private bathrooms, impeccably appointed, are no less impressive. Equipped with a rejuvenating shower and luxury bathtub, a hairdryer, and a selection of high-end complimentary toiletries, offering a sanctuary for relaxation and restoration after a day exploring the vibrant city of Oviedo. Moreover, in an era when staying connected is imperative, the Hotel de la Reconquista provides complimentary WiFi access throughout the property, ensuring guests can remain in touch with the outside world or simply share their unforgettable experiences with friends and family.

Delaney found himself in a world of timeless elegance and modern convenience, set against the backdrop of Oviedo's rich history and vibrant culture. As he settled into his room, he couldn't help but appreciate the seamless blend of the past and present that the Hotel de la Reconquista offered, making his stay not only comfortable but also an opportunity to immerse himself in the city's captivating ambiance.

With a casual glance at his watch, he made a deliberate choice to surrender to the soothing embrace of relaxation for a short time after his arduous journey.

Oviedo, a city rich in history and culture, beckoned to him, promising an array of captivating sights and experiences. Delaney was not here to unwind but to embark on the initial stages of unraveling the enigmatic puzzle surrounding the heist of the Sudarium of Oviedo. However, being a tourist would help him focus.

His first outing was a leisurely exploration of the city's myriad attractions, each a portal into Oviedo's fascinating story. As he meandered through the medieval cobblestone streets, the intricate architecture and vibrant street life drew him in, offering glimpses of both ancient traditions and contemporary flair. The aroma of local delicacies wafted through the air, igniting his senses and inviting him to savor the culinary wonders that Oviedo had to offer.

Yet, his underlying mission remained a constant companion. His destination, the Cathedral of San Salvador, stood as a symbol of both spiritual sanctity and, in his case, a crime scene. It was here that Delaney's analytical mind went to work, meticulously studying the exterior of the cathedral. With a keen eye for detail, he scrutinized the structure, its architectural elements, and any signs that might reveal the modus operandi of the audacious heist that had unfolded within its sacred confines.

While he understood that solving this intricate puzzle would be a formidable task, Delaney was undaunted. His determination and analytical prowess would be the guiding forces behind every step of the investigation. As he took in the city's charm and began his examination of the cathedral, he felt a sense of purpose and anticipation, knowing that he was on the precipice of a thrilling journey that would take him deeper into the heart of the mystery.

Opting for an early dinner, Delaney made his way to the Dona Concha restaurant, conveniently situated within a stone's throw of a charming church. With a welcoming ambiance and an enticing menu, it was the perfect spot for an evening of gastronomic exploration.

As he settled into his seat, an assortment of delectable cheeses arrived at his table, accompanied by freshly baked sourdough bread and a tantalizing bowl of vinegar and olive oil. The delightful combination of flavors and textures danced on his palate, setting the stage for what promised to be a memorable meal.

After this delectable appetizer, Delaney decided to savor the house specialty, the confit cod, which was expertly prepared and served alongside charcoal-grilled leeks. To complete the culinary experience, he indulged in a bowl of Oricios stew, an offering that perfectly encapsulated the region's flavors.

As the meal reached its satisfying conclusion, Delaney chose to forgo dessert in favor of a glass of Spanish wine. While the specific name of the wine eluded his memory, its rich and velvety notes provided a fitting finish to a sumptuous dinner. The evening at Dona Concha delighted his taste buds and offered a glimpse into Oviedo's culinary treasures, leaving him with a sense of contentment and appreciation for the city's gastronomic offerings.

He arrived at the cathedral at 9 a.m. under an assumed name selected by his agency for a pre-arranged meeting with the hierarchy of the cathedral and a member of the Vatican security force, who had remained at the site of the theft.

Before venturing inside, Delaney paused to fully immerse himself in the breathtaking beauty of the Cathedral of San Salvador of Oviedo. The magnificent edifice presented a captivating tapestry of architectural styles, offering a visual journey through the ages. It was as if the cathedral whispered the secrets of Oviedo's history through its meticulously crafted stone, embodying a timeless fusion of artistic mastery and spiritual significance.

The cathedral's exterior was a testament to an enduring architectural legacy, featuring elements from Pre-Romanesque to Baroque, a span that encompassed the Romanesque, Gothic, and Renaissance periods. This remarkable diversity of styles told a vivid tale of the city's evolving identity, with each section of the cathedral serving as a chapter in this architectural narrative.

The Pre-Romanesque elements, characterized by clean lines and minimal ornamentation, reflected Oviedo's early history, offering a glimpse into the city's formative years. The Romanesque portions of the cathedral showcased the artistry of the medieval period, with intricate arches, columns, and carvings that conveyed a sense of religious devotion.

Moving into the Gothic sections, the cathedral's architecture soared to new heights, both literally and figuratively. Ribbed vaults, towering spires, and ornate stained-glass windows brought a sense of grandeur and spirituality to the forefront, creating an awe-inspiring atmosphere that resonated with the divine.

The Renaissance elements of the cathedral added a touch of classicism with symmetrical designs and graceful proportions. These sections represented a period of rebirth and cultural enlightenment, contributing to the ever-evolving character of the magnificent building.

As Delaney gazed at the exterior, the intricate interplay of architectural styles painted a vivid picture of Oviedo's history and its enduring connection to faith and art. It was a tangible link to the city's past, a testament to the architects, craftsmen, and artisans who had dedicated their skills and creativity to this spiritual masterpiece.

As he walked amidst the architectural grandeur of the Cathedral of San Salvador of Oviedo, Delaney was acutely aware of the weight of history pressing upon him. The cathedral's awe-inspiring presence seemed to evoke an almost spiritual reverence, prompting his mind to meander down the lanes of memory and reflection. It was at this moment that his thoughts turned, like pages from a forgotten chapter, to Jeannie, his former lover.

His initial contemplation centered on the deep remorse he harbored for the way he had vanished from their once-cherished relationship. He couldn't help but feel the gravity of his actions, knowing that Jeannie had loved him with a fervor that he had inadequately reciprocated. He had concealed his darker, more enigmatic side from her, never fully allowing her into the shadowy corners of his life. Rather than facing his demons and exposing his soul to her, he had chosen the path of abrupt departure, believing that a clean break would be kinder in the end despite the inevitable heartache it would cause.

Delaney's mind traversed a dark and clandestine narrative in the recesses of his thoughts, revealing a chapter of his life that he had long kept buried. His enigmatic new employer had orchestrated his supposed 'death' during a high-stakes mission. The mission had entailed dismantling the urban terrorist organization known as the Black Cell, a group that had audaciously plunged a portion of the Super Bowl into darkness with insidious plans to push the world's superpowers to the brink of nuclear conflict. Their ultimate aim was to harness the chaos they had sown and exploit it for their gain by hacking into the world's largest bank.

During the operation, the Black Cell had booby-trapped an abandoned nuclear silo with explosives, resulting in a catastrophic detonation that claimed the lives of several of Delaney's comrades. His enigmatic employer seized this tragedy as an opportunity, orchestrating a staged 'death' for Delaney. This elaborate ruse afforded him a clean slate, free from his past, his former life, and, most painfully, Jeannie.

As he stood before the cathedral, grappling with these haunting memories and the profound sense of loss they evoked, Delaney couldn't help but wonder if he would ever find the redemption and closure he so desperately sought or if his past would continue to cast a long shadow over his ambiguous existence.

Delaney had silently assisted Jeannie from the shadows as she had tirelessly pursued the elusive trail of the missing Hitler clone and the sinister designs of The Organization, aimed at reviving the ghost of the Fourth Reich. His covert involvement took the form of a series of anonymous letters discreetly dispatched to the FBI bureau in San Francisco. These missives contained valuable information and leads for Jeannie to follow, allowing her to piece together the complex puzzle.

Delaney remained uncertain whether Jeannie had ever connected the dots and realized that he was the anonymous benefactor still operating from the shadows. The enigma of his continued existence was a riddle he was resigned to never solving.

Yet, as he contemplated his motives for rekindling his connection with Jeannie, a surge of recognition washed over Delaney as he remembered that Jeannie's unique and profound knowledge of art history could prove invaluable in deciphering the complex web of clues and secrets that lay before him.

In that moment, a spark of realization ignited within him, shedding light on the untapped potential that Jeannie represented in the intricate case he now faced. She was not just his former lover, she was also a formidable asset in unraveling the mysteries of the past and the impending challenges that awaited.

With this revelation, he vowed to keep the thought of Jeannie as a valuable resource tucked away in the recesses of his mind, ready to call upon her expertise should the need arise. In the intricate chess game that lay ahead, he recognized that Jeannie's unique insights might be the key to checkmating the enigmatic foe they were both determined to face.

CHAPTER ELEVEN

Jeannie arrived at Dr. Goldsmith's office promptly for her scheduled appointment. Her relief was palpable when she noticed that only two other patients occupied the waiting room. She sat and filled out the medical forms provided on a clipboard, a customary ritual before a doctor's consultation. Her eyes roamed the room as she patiently waited, taking in the nondescript décor and the sterile atmosphere that seemed to define the space.

The moment of truth came when she was ushered into a small examination room. As she perched on the uncomfortable examination table, memories of previous medical appointments and procedures swirled through her mind. The setting felt vaguely reminiscent of a GYN exam room, a thought she quickly dismissed. Fortunately, her visit today was not of that nature.

Dr. Goldsmith entered. He was completely bald, with reading glasses dangling from a strap and resting on his chest. He approached carrying Jeannie's chart, offering a warm greeting. "Hello, Ms. Loomis. I'm Dr. Goldsmith. Nice to meet you," he said, preparing to sit on a small rolling stool. With a casual movement, he pushed his glasses up to his brow, a signal that he was about to delve into her medical history.

Jeannie acknowledged the doctor's introduction with a nod. "Dr. Shelby indicated that you have been experiencing a series of debilitating headaches and that the prescribed medication isn't bringing relief," Dr. Goldsmith observed.

"Yes," Jeannie confirmed. "They've become less frequent, but the pain is excruciating when they strike."

Dr. Goldsmith maintained his gaze on Jeannie for a moment before flashing a friendly smile. "Treating a highly decorated FBI agent is a first for me."

Jeannie couldn't help but smile back, appreciating the doctor's attempt at lightening the mood. "Well, I'll take that as a compliment, doctor, but this FBI agent is starting to feel the weight of aging."

They shared a chuckle, easing the tension in the room. However, it was evident that Dr. Goldsmith had a significant revelation to make, and Jeannie's intuition hinted at the gravity of the news that was about to unfold.

"Ms. Loomis," he began, but Jeannie interrupted, urging him to use her first name. "Please, Doctor, call me Jeannie."

"Jeannie it is," Dr. Goldsmith agreed. He then inquired about the presence of anyone accompanying her to the appointment. Her mind immediately raced, anticipating further tests. "Do you have anyone here with you today?"

A sense of concern gripped Jeannie as she pondered the implications of his question. "No, are you planning additional tests? If so, I could arrange for an Uber driver to take me home and return for my car later."

Dr. Goldsmith shook his head gently, assuaging her worries. "No, that won't be necessary, Jeannie. Unfortunately, your MRI scan has revealed the presence of a tumor in your temporal lobe." He raised the scan, pointing to a circle he had drawn around the ominous mass. He paused, gauging her reaction, acutely aware of the weight of his words.

Jeannie's concern deepened as she leaned forward to see the circle on the MRI. "And the prognosis?" she inquired, her voice tinged with trepidation.

Dr. Goldsmith maintained a composed demeanor as he elaborated, "Well, I prefer not to make assumptions. We'll need to conduct a biopsy to determine the nature of the tumor."

The word 'biopsy' hit Jeannie like a thunderbolt, and Jeannie felt a surge of anxiety. "A biopsy? That sounds quite serious, Doctor."

Dr. Goldsmith adopted a reassuring tone, seeking to allay her fears. "Indeed, we've made significant advancements in biopsy procedures. In your case, we're referring to a stereotactic brain biopsy, which takes place in an operating room under strictly sterile conditions. The procedure is carried out under general anesthesia, although in some cases, it can be performed under sedation. Most patients opt for the former. The entire procedure usually takes less than an hour. However, due to our hospital policies and liability considerations, you will require someone to accompany you to the hospital and take you home."

Jeannie nodded, absorbing the information, her thoughts already racing ahead to her challenging medical journey.

"When can we arrange for the procedure?" Jeannie inquired anxiously, her concern for her health fueling her desire for a swift examination and potential treatment of the tumor.

Dr. Goldsmith offered a reassuring nod. "I'll have my scheduling nurse prioritize your appointment and get you in as soon as possible. In the interim, I'd like to add one more medication to what Dr. Shelby has already prescribed. While this won't cure the tumor, it should provide relief for the pain, vertigo, and other symptoms you're experiencing until we can proceed with the necessary intervention."

Jeannie's drive home from Dr. Goldsmith's office was a blur. Overwhelmed by a torrent of fear and apprehension, she grappled with the seriousness that now loomed before her. The weight of this medical challenge was too heavy for one person to bear alone, and this realization presented a series of pressing concerns.

The question of who to confide in gnawed at her thoughts. She pondered her dilemma as the miles passed by unnoticed. Jeannie knew she couldn't shoulder this burden in isolation. As her mind swirled with uncertainty, she hesitated to press Dr. Goldsmith for details on his suspicions regarding the nature of the tumor. It was a fine line to walk, as she didn't want to jump to conclusions, but practicality had always guided her actions. She had often heard her stepfather's sage advice echoing in her mind, "Prepare for the worst so you're not caught off guard."

As she navigated the uncertain medical road ahead, Jeannie understood that she needed to share her journey with someone, lean on their support, and face the challenges that lay ahead together. The isolation she felt during the drive home only reinforced her conviction to reach out and find solace in the strength of others.

"Good morning, Father," Delaney greeted with a warm smile, extending his hand in a gesture of respect. "I'm Agent Richard Trotter of Interpol. I'm here to meet with Father Marino."

Delaney was amazed at how easy it was to lie to people and assume a false name.

"Good morning, Agent Trotter. I'm Father Marino," replied the priest with a heavy Italian accent, returning the handshake. "We have been anticipating your arrival. Please, come in."

As they stepped through the grand entrance of the Cathedral of San Salvador, Delaney couldn't help but marvel at the breathtaking beauty that surrounded him. The interior was a symphony of divine artistry, with towering arches that seemed to reach for the heavens, stained glass windows that bathed the sacred space in a kaleidoscope of colors, and intricately carved details that adorned every inch.

The soft sunlight filtered in through the windows, casting a warm, ethereal glow on the polished marble floors. Delicate whispers of incense lingered in the air, creating an atmosphere of reverence and serenity. The sacred ambiance of the cathedral resonated with a timeless grace that captivated the senses.

Father Marino led Agent Trotter through the hallowed halls, their footsteps echoing in the vast expanse. As they approached the altar, Delaney couldn't help but be drawn to the cathedral's historical significance, especially its connection to the Sudarium, the relic of immense importance that once found its sanctuary within these sacred walls.

The Cathedral of San Salvador stood as a testament to centuries of faith and devotion, its architectural grandeur and artistic richness telling a story of divine worship. Delaney couldn't help but feel a sense of awe and reverence, realizing that this was not just a place of worship but also a living repository of history and spirituality.

As they moved deeper into the heart of the cathedral, Delaney's eyes were drawn to the intricacies of the artwork that adorned the walls and ceilings. Each stroke of paint, each carefully crafted sculpture, seemed to whisper tales of devotion and artistic brilliance. It was as if the very essence of faith had been immortalized in the stones and canvases that adorned the sacred space.

As they reached the chamber that once cradled the Sudarium, the air seemed to thicken with a sense of mystery and history. The emptiness left by the relic's theft echoed in the quiet chambers, magnifying the gravity of the situation. Delaney knew that uncovering the truth would not only be a pursuit of justice but also a journey into the heart of a place that held the whispers of centuries gone by—the Cathedral of San Salvador, a timeless testament to faith, beauty, and the human spirit.

The duo stepped into a cozy chamber nestled on the side of the grand cathedral, where they were met by a second priest. "This is Father Ricci. Father, meet Interpol Agent Trotter."

Father Ricci rose from his seat, extending a hand with a warm smile. He greeted Delaney in an Italian accent similar to Father Marino's, "I hope your journey to Oviedo was without incident." The three settled into a comfortable arrangement, forming a small circle within the room.

"Yes, fortunately, my arrival allowed me the rest of the day to explore the city, and I must say, I was thoroughly impressed," Delaney shared before steering the conversation toward the purpose of their meeting. "So, could you both enlighten me on what transpired? I understand you've recounted the events before, but I've often found that with time, certain details that may have been overlooked tend to resurface."

Before Father Ricci or Father Mahoney uttered a word, a tall, slender gentleman with jet-black, slicked-back hair entered the room, clad in a stylish blue suit adorned with a matching tie. His gaze fixed on Delaney, and he approached with purposeful strides. Delaney rose to his feet, and the two exchanged a firm handshake as the newcomer introduced himself. "I'm Antonio Moretti," he declared, his voice carrying an Italian cadence. "I represent the Vatican security force in the investigation of the Sudarium theft and the unfortunate murder of Father Marchetti. It brings me great satisfaction to learn that Interpol is now collaborating with us in this crucial inquiry."

"Pleasure to make your acquaintance. I'm Richard Trotter," Delaney responded with a cordial smile. "As I've discussed with Father Mahoney and Father Ricci, I understand that Interpol has entered the investigation at a late stage, and numerous interviews have already been conducted. However, I believe it's beneficial for everyone to undergo a reinterview. With the passage of time, certain details that may have eluded discovery early on tend to come to light."

"I agree," Moretti concurred. "Maybe, Father," he turned his attention to Mahoney, "we could arrange for some refreshments."

Without uttering a word, Father Mahoney stood up and exited the gathering. "Now, how would you prefer to proceed?" Moretti inquired, turning his attention back to Delaney.

CHAPTER TWELVE

Upon Father Mahoney's return, the group indulged in some coffee and pastries. "So, who would like to kick things off by sharing when the crime was first discovered? Once I have that foundation, I can chart the course for the rest of my inquiry," Delaney proposed.

The two fathers exchanged glances, tacitly agreeing that Father Ricci would be the one to commence. "It was around 5 p.m. when I started my routine walk from my bedroom to the cathedral, as I've been doing since my assignment from the Vatican. I immediately spotted Father Marchetti lying on the floor," Father Ricci began, making the sign of the cross before continuing.

"At first, I thought he might have taken a fall, but then I noticed the pool of blood beneath his head and his fixed stare. I called out for assistance, and Father Mahoney arrived. While he examined Father Marchetti, I went to the usual area where the Sudarium is stored and discovered it was missing," Father Ricci explained, casting a glance toward Father Mahoney, who seamlessly took over.

"It was evident that Father Marchetti had been murdered. I promptly contacted the authorities and took measures to secure the area, restricting anyone else from entering, including the room that housed the Sudarium. Simultaneously, I made a call to the Vatican and started the process for Mr. Moretti's arrival," Father Mahoney added, providing a seamless transition in the narrative.

"I understand. Now, my next set of questions may delve into some uncomfortable territory, and I appreciate having you here, Mr. Moretti, representing the Vatican security force. I'll be focusing on the security measures that were in effect leading up to the Sudarium's theft," Delaney explained, sensing a subtle unease in all three individuals associated with the church. Both Father Mahoney and Father Ricci turned to Mr. Moretti, seeking guidance on how much information to disclose.

Before they could respond, Moretti stepped in. "Agent Trotter, my directive comes directly from the Holy Father himself, and it is to offer you any necessary information and assistance to facilitate the retrieval of the holy relic. Perhaps, as a starting point, a tour of the cathedral, beginning in the room where it was normally housed, would be beneficial. We can then elaborate on the various security systems that were in place."

Forty-five minutes after an extensive tour and a thorough examination of the intricate security system safeguarding the Sudarium, Delaney found himself standing in contemplation. The cathedral's security measures were, as anticipated, state-of-the-art—impenetrable to an ordinary thief. Every layer of protection seemed meticulously designed to ensure the sanctity of the holy relic. However, as Delaney absorbed the details, a realization settled within him like a growing storm.

The sophistication of the security system led him to a troubling deduction: there had to be an insider, someone intimately familiar with the cathedral's defenses. The precision with which the perpetrators had executed the theft indicated a level of knowledge that transcended what an external observer could attain. It was a disconcerting revelation, suggesting a breach of trust within the cathedral's sacred walls. Father Marchetti's appearance was an obstacle the thief or thieves had not anticipated, but that was immediately resolved with his murder.

As Delaney mulled over this disquieting realization, he couldn't help but wonder about the motives and allegiances of those involved. The betrayal, if his suspicions proved correct, added a layer of complexity to the investigation. The cathedral, a symbol of faith and spiritual solace, now harbored secrets that went beyond the physical realm. Determined to unravel the truth, Delaney knew he had to navigate not only the external challenges but also the shadows within, where trust had been fractured, and the pursuit of justice demanded a delicate balance between faith and scrutiny.

"Agent Trotter, you appear deep in thought," Moretti observed, his inquiry hanging in the air, accompanied by the watchful gazes of Fathers Mahoney and Ricci.

Startled from his reverie, Delaney redirected his attention to the trio before him. In that moment, he grappled with the delicate task of broaching the unsettling notion that had lodged in his mind—a suspicion that pointed toward an inside job. There seemed to be no alternative explanation for the seamless execution of the theft.

With a measured gaze, Delaney weighed his words, considering the impact of his revelation on the clergy standing before him. The cathedral, a haven of faith, now found itself entangled in a web of deceit. Despite the solemnity of the surroundings, the truth demanded acknowledgment.

"Mr. Moretti, Fathers Mahoney and Ricci," Delaney began cautiously, "I can't help but wonder about the level of sophistication displayed in this theft. The security measures are undoubtedly state-of-the-art, and yet, it seems as though the perpetrators had an uncanny knowledge of the cathedral's defenses. It begs the question: was there someone on the inside assisting them?" The gravity of his words hung in the air, casting a shadow over the sacred space as the implications of a breach of trust unfurled.

Moretti's gaze shifted between the uneasy priests, their discomfort evident in the solemn air. "Agent Trotter," he began with a measured tone, "the Vatican, based on my investigation, aligns with your premise. Regrettably, it appears that someone from within the cathedral was involved in the theft of the Sudarium. The Vatican aims to handle this matter with the utmost confidentiality, keeping the information tightly controlled and away from the public eye. I trust you comprehend the sensitivity of the situation?"

"Understood," Delaney replied, his expression serious as he absorbed the weight of the revelation. "Given this understanding, the question now becomes: who within the cathedral possessed the sensitive information that facilitated the Sudarium's theft?" Delaney's eyes fixed on Moretti, a determination to unravel the mystery evident in his look.

"Mr. Moretti, I request that you provide me with the names of individuals who had access to the crucial details necessary for the thieves to carry out this operation successfully," Delaney continued, his tone unwavering. The sacred trust had been violated, and it was imperative to identify the culprit or culprits who had betrayed the sanctuary of faith.

Moretti nodded solemnly, acknowledging the critical nature of the matter. "Agent Trotter, our investigation has been ongoing, and we have been diligently working to identify the individual or individuals responsible. The name that surfaces most prominently as a suspect is Brother Giuseppe Renaldi. He held a position within the cathedral that granted him access to the inner workings and security protocols. Unfortunately, he has vanished without a trace since the theft, making our efforts to locate him challenging."

Delaney absorbed this information, his mind racing to formulate the next steps in the pursuit of justice. The trail was leading to a vanished suspect, adding a layer of complexity to an already intricate investigation. The echoes of betrayal reverberated within the hallowed walls, and the path forward demanded a delicate balance between unraveling the truth and preserving the sanctity of faith.

CHAPTER THIRTEEN

The biopsy procedure spanned approximately two hours, factoring in the pre-requirements that Jeannie needed to undergo beforehand. In adherence to the hospital's protocol, which mandated that patients have a relative accompany them for transportation, Jeannie had taken a strategic approach. She went above and beyond, compensating an Uber driver generously—well beyond the standard fare. The driver not only patiently waited for her throughout the procedure but also assumed the role of her brother, ensuring compliance with the hospital's transportation policy. She was told she would be notified of the results by her doctor in a few days.

On Monday, Jeannie found herself feeling a bit better and on the path to recovery, so she decided to drive to work. Wary of reassuring her concerned co-workers about her well-being, she settled into her office chair, anticipating the lively banter that would follow with Ismail's arrival. As if on cue, he strolled in, bearing a cup of coffee for Jeannie and a tempting chocolate donut.

"I figure you need to keep up your strength since you're getting old and everything," Ismail quipped, attempting to suppress a laugh.

"Your bedside manner sucks, but thanks a ton for the coffee and refreshments. Now, spill the beans on the diamond heist in Burlingame. Any progress? Have you ruled out the security officers?" Jeannie inquired, her curiosity piqued.

"Yeah, they all submitted to polygraphs and passed with flying colors. I'm leaning toward the theory that it's an inside job, perhaps an insurance rip-off," Ismail shared, his eyes reflecting a blend of seriousness and deduction.

"Huh," Jeannie responded thoughtfully, taking a bite of the donut and washing it down with a satisfying sip of coffee. The tantalizing combination of chocolate and caffeine provided a momentary distraction from the weightier matters at hand.

"So, boss, how are the headaches?" Ismail prodded with genuine concern. "You know, a stiff drink of Portuguese red wine might just do the trick," he grinned, offering a playful solution to alleviate the lingering effects of her recent ordeal.

Just as Jeannie was about to pick up the banter with Ismail, SAC Lomax entered her office, his presence bringing a temporary pause to the playful exchange. "I assume you're feeling better?" he inquired, acknowledging the recent challenges Jeannie had faced.

"Much better, thanks. Now, spill the beans—how's the transfer of Agent Ismail Flores to Fairbanks, Alaska going?"

"I'm right here," Ismail chimed in, a smile playing on his face as he anticipated the response.

SAC Lomax, however, maintained a straight face. "Not going to happen. They're looking for a much younger agent," he deadpanned, adding a touch of humor to the unexpected revelation. Ismail chuckled, appreciating the banter despite the playful jibe at his age.

"Since you're both present," Lomax shifted gears to delve into more weighty subjects, "I must bring to your attention that the State Department has specifically sought your collaboration with Interpol on a case pertaining to the theft of a highly significant religious relic."

"The Sudarium?" inquired Jeannie.

"The very same. Are you acquainted with this relic?" Lomax inquired.

"Yes, I took several art history classes during my undergraduate studies, and relics such as the Sudarium, the Shroud of Turin, and the True Cross always held a captivating fascination for me."

"Sorry, I don't know any of the items Jeannie just mentioned," Ismail said.

"When you start getting older, your memory is one of the first things you lose," Lomax said, grinning at Jeannie, who laughed.

"Very funny," Ismail replied. "So, we need to check in with Interpol?"

"Interestingly, the Vatican specifically requested you two for this task. I don't have all the particulars yet, but I just got off the phone with Washington, and you are to head to the Interpol office as soon as possible. There, you'll be briefed on the details."

"The Vatican?" Jeannie asked. "I can see the connection between the Vatican and Interpol, but how did Ismail and I get dragged into this?"

"I wish I had more information for you, but I'm sure Interpol has more background on how this came about," Lomax responded. The unexpected turn of events added an air of mystery to the day, setting the stage for a new and compelling mission.

Vincent D'Amico reassembled his crew since the date for the theft of the Shroud of Turin was nearing. This would be their final meeting in his castle before they left for Turin, Italy, in twenty-four hours. The main purpose of the meeting was for Natalia to report on the insider information she had learned in the hopes of defeating the security measures in place.

For the past several weeks, Natalia had been using her captivating charm to seduce the main person responsible for the Shroud's security. In the dimly lit corner of a lavish penthouse, the cunning and beautiful villain leaned against a mahogany table, her piercing gaze locked onto James Hartfield, the security expert with intimate knowledge of the protective measures surrounding the revered Shroud of Turin.

She first met him when he was giving a lecture on the history of the Shroud of Turin. After purposely bumping into him and spilling her drink, a relationship developed as she had planned.

Natalia's crimson lips curled into a sly smile as she sipped from a crystal glass, the amber liquid reflecting the flickering candlelight. Her gown allowed her to display her ample cleavage, something that James could not keep his roaming eyes off.

"James," she purred, her voice dripping with seduction, "I've always been fascinated by the art of security, the delicate dance between safeguarding and infiltration. Rumor has it you're the virtuoso in charge of protecting the Shroud of Turin."

James, captivated by Natalia's magnetic presence, couldn't help but feel a thrill run down his spine. "Well, I don't usually discuss my work," he replied cautiously, his eyes betraying a hint of curiosity as he moved closer to Natalia.

Natalia took a step closer, her stiletto heels clicking softly on the polished marble floor. "Oh, James, you don't have to be so formal with me. I've heard whispers about the layers of bulletproof glass cocooning that precious relic. I can't help but wonder how such an exquisite masterpiece is safeguarded."

As she spoke, Natalia delicately traced her fingertips along the edge of a sleek touchscreen tablet that James had brought with him that contained the Shroud's security protocols. Unbeknownst to him, she was expertly scanning the intricate details that would pave the way for their unholy heist.

James, drawn into Natalia's magnetic charm, began to divulge more than he intended. "The glass is reinforced with a cutting-edge polymer composite, layered to withstand even the most advanced attempts at intrusion. Access points are limited and guarded with state-of-the-art biometric scanners. It's a fortress, really."

Natalia's eyes gleamed with satisfaction as she absorbed every detail, filing away the information for her nefarious plans. "How utterly fascinating," she whispered, her warm breath caressing James's ear. "I would love to hear more about the vulnerabilities and perhaps explore them further in the privacy of my own sanctuary."

Lost in a haze of passion and oblivious to the impending danger, James was entirely consumed by Natalia's allure. As the evening unfolded, he failed to notice the subtle introduction of a date-rape drug into his champagne glass, a sinister touch orchestrated by the beguiling Natalia. Oblivious, he succumbed to the drug's effects, his senses dulled as Natalia skillfully guided him to the expansive king-size bed.

With calculated grace, Natalia began a seductive dance, slowly shedding her gown to reveal the tantalizing silhouette of her lingerie. James, struggling to maintain focus, found his efforts futile as a drowsy lethargy overcame him, eventually lulling him into a deep and involuntary slumber.

Seizing the opportunity, Natalia swiftly restored her dress, her attention now turned to James's belongings. She deftly retrieved his iPad, a tool that held the gateway to the secrets she sought. Luckily, James had left several files open, eliminating the need for a password. Natalia urgently perused the digital documents until she uncovered the crucial information—the procedure for deactivating the security measures safeguarding the Shroud.

Armed with her cell phone, Natalia clandestinely captured images of the sensitive documents, securing a record of the critical steps needed for her sinister plot. Satisfied with her haul, she returned to the last file James had previewed, leaving no digital trace of her intrusion.

Turning her attention back to the unconscious James, Natalia skillfully removed every article of his clothing, meticulously placing them at the foot of the bed. A touch of audacity took hold as she snatched a piece of stationary from a nearby desk, pressing her lips against it to leave behind a provocative kiss-shaped imprint. Placing the token of her audacious act on the pillow beside James, she envisioned his inevitable discovery once the effects of the drug wore off.

Certain she had covered her tracks, Natalia, shrouded in the shadows of her deceit, silently departed, leaving James vulnerable and unknowingly paving the way for the impending turmoil in the narrative of their tangled fates.

CHAPTER FOURTEEN

Delaney lay on his hotel bed, his gaze fixed on the ceiling, as he pondered his next move and contemplated whether his suggestion to involve Jeannie in the investigation had been set in motion by his director. His cell phone, resting beside him, suddenly vibrated. Glancing at the caller ID, he recognized the number; it was his supervisor.

"Sean, I bring you two pieces of good news. First, the Pope has agreed that Agent Loomis should join the investigation. She'll reach out to your former office in San Francisco, likely today or tomorrow. Now, on a more pressing matter, we've managed to triangulate the location of your missing Brother, Giuseppe Renaldi. It seems he's on the run but has halted in Tuscany. I'll send you the coordinates. Happy hunting."

Delaney skillfully arranged a journey across countries, orchestrating a flight from the vibrant city of Barcelona, Spain, to the enchanting Tuscan landscapes of Florence, Italy, all through the seamless medium of a telephone conversation. With the prospect of an extensive expedition ahead, he clung to the optimistic notion that Brother Renaldi, for some fortuitous reason, would linger in the picturesque region of Tuscany until Delaney's arrival.

After a prolonged taxi drive, Delaney found himself in the heart of Tuscany. Instead of prioritizing the customary check-in ritual at a hotel, his immediate focus was pinpointing Brother Renaldi's whereabouts. Delaney, armed with the geographical coordinates provided to him, adeptly identified a hotel nestled in a corner of the city. Opting for a strategic position, he settled into an outdoor café that afforded him a panoramic view of the hotel's entrance and exit.

Immersing himself in the ambiance of the city, Delaney savored a leisurely interlude of forty-five minutes, sipping on rich Italian coffee and indulging in delectable pastries. His patient vigilance was rewarded when he observed Brother Renaldi emerging from the hotel, accompanied by another male, both burdened with luggage.

Showing his gratitude for the café's hospitality, Delaney left his payment with a generous tip before embarking on a discreet pursuit of the duo. Renaldi and his companion hailed a cab, prompting Delaney to swiftly replicate their actions, trailing them to the bustling railroad station.

After settling the taxi fare, Delaney proceeded to tail the duo on foot, ultimately reaching a busy ticket station. Maintaining a discreet distance, he overheard their chosen destination and promptly acquired a ticket for himself, ensuring seamless integration into their journey. In due course, the train pulled into the station, and from a prudent distance, Delaney boarded behind the two. Carefully trailing them, he eventually arrived at their train car, nonchalantly passing by as they made their way through the compartment. Now, the waiting game began.

As the train slowly departed from the terminal, a porter navigated the corridor, diligently rapping on each compartment door to verify passengers' tickets. Methodically making his way through the carriages, the porter eventually reached the cabin occupied by Brother Renaldi and his companion. Following the ticket check, the companion exited the cabin, leaving Brother Renaldi alone. This serendipitous turn of events was precisely what Delaney had been hoping for.

Capitalizing on the opportune moment, Delaney approached the cabin door and gave a distinct knock, announcing, "Tickets." Brother Renaldi responded, with a hint of irritation in his expression, "We already showed you our tickets."

Undeterred, Delaney forcefully pushed the door open, inadvertently striking Renaldi in the face and causing his nose to bleed. Acting swiftly, Delaney closed and locked the door behind him, his demeanor now intense. Exposing a suppressed firearm, he gestured for Renaldi to take a seat at the small table near the window.

The confined space of the cabin was tense as, with a stern expression, Delaney took control of the situation. The subdued sounds of the train picking up speed served as an eerie backdrop to the unfolding events within the compartment.

"Brother Renaldi," Delaney asserted, adopting a direct approach, "I'll cut to the chase, as the Americans say. You were involved in the theft of the Sudarium from the cathedral. Now, I want to know who hired you and the current whereabouts of the relic."

A look of feigned innocence washed over Renaldi's face as he responded, "You must be mistaken. I am not this Brother Renaldi. I don't know who he is. My name is Peter Maldova."

Unconvinced and undeterred, Delaney responded with swift and forceful action, using the butt of his handgun to strike Renaldi's nose once again. This time, the impact was undeniable, as the brother's nose visibly broke, releasing a fresh stream of blood down his chin.

"I'm not certain how much time we have before your companion returns," Delaney declared coldly. "If he shows up before you provide me with the information I seek, I'll let him enter and shoot him in the head. The choice is entirely yours. Shall we try this again? Who hired you, and where is the Sudarium?" The intensity in Delaney's gaze matched the urgency of the situation, hanging in the claustrophobic cabin.

Delaney raised the gun menacingly, creating a palpable tension in the cramped space. In a reflexive defense, Brother Renaldi lifted his hands, his eyes betraying a mixture of fear and desperation.

"Please. Alright. I will tell you," Renaldi acquiesced under the ominous threat. "A woman approached me one afternoon while I was having lunch. We chatted for a while until she abruptly pulled out her cellphone, revealing a series of pictures."

Delaney, fixated on extracting the crucial information, interrupted, "And these pictures were of what?" Silence filled the air, prompting Delaney to wave the gun again, emphasizing the graveness of the situation.

Renaldi, his gaze fixed on the floor, eventually spoke, "They were pictures of me with some children." A sense of shame colored his admission. "She told me that if I didn't provide her with the information she sought, those pictures would be plastered all over the Internet and sent to the Vatican."

The gravity of this revelation settled around them as Delaney grappled with the moral quandary that Brother Renaldi found himself ensnared in. Delaney's struggle to obtain information took on a darker and more complex dimension.

"Does this woman have a name?" Delaney probed insistently.

" I remember her name was Natalia," Renaldi divulged.

Delaney pressed further, his curiosity undeterred. "And what does this Natalia look like?"

Renaldi recounted, "She is a very beautiful woman with a distinct Russian accent. Long black hair frames her face, and her eyes carry an air of mystery. I don't know how else to describe her." Renaldi's recollection painted a vivid image of Natalia. "While we spoke, she exhibited a directness that revealed her extensive knowledge about the Sudarium and the cathedral. I instantly grasped what she was after and began to rise from the table where we were seated."

He paused, letting his narrative sink in. "But she shook her head, indicating no. That's when she revealed, under her cloth napkin, a gun pointed directly at me. It was a chilling moment and a clear signal that compliance was not optional." The tension in Renaldi's voice mirrored the harrowing encounter he'd had with Natalia, underscoring the dangerous game in which he had become an unwitting participant.

"What did she say exactly?" Delaney pressed, his focus unwavering.

Renaldi closed his eyes as if shutting out the present moment would aid his recollection. "She said she had a very wealthy buyer who desired to expand his collection of holy relics. Natalia assured me that no harm would befall the Sudarium, emphasizing that her buyer already had a special container prepared for the relic once it was in his possession."

A troubled expression crossed Renaldi's face as he continued, "Then, she asked for specifics, warning me that if the theft did not proceed as planned, she would meticulously track me down, and…" he hesitated, the unspoken threat lingering in the air. The weight of Natalia's ominous words hung heavy in the small train cabin, underscoring the perilous stakes involved with the mysterious pursuit of the sacred artifact.

"So, you provided her with inside information regarding the Sudarium's security?" Delaney inquired, his scrutiny unwavering.

Renaldi nodded reluctantly. "Yes. She took out a small tape recorder and had me describe in meticulous detail all the security systems in place and how to deactivate them."

"And then?" Delaney probed further. "She just got up and left the table?"

"No," Renaldi replied, a hint of surprise in his voice. "Surprisingly, she reached into her purse and pulled out an envelope, sliding it across the table to me. I opened it and found thousands of Euros inside. She told me that my religious career was over and that I should seriously consider relocating from Spain. My friend and I were attempting that when you found me."

"Did she ever disclose who the buyer was?" Delaney asked, seeking the missing pieces of the puzzle.

Renaldi closed his eyes momentarily, trying to recall. "Wait. Yes. While discussing the buyer and the elaborate steps he had taken to ensure the proper safekeeping of the relic, she mentioned Vincent but no last name. What will happen to me now?"

Delaney paused with a thoughtful expression on his face. "I suggest that you heed Natalia's advice about relocating but consider Eastern Europe or the United States as better destinations than your current trajectory."

Rising from his seat, Delaney straightened his tie and jacket, securing the handgun in a shoulder harness. Without exchanging final words, he unlocked the cabin door and left, leaving Renaldi to grapple with the consequences of his involvement in the shadowy world of stolen relics and clandestine dealings. The train rattled on, carrying with it the weight of secrets and Renaldi's uncertain future.

CHAPTER FIFTEEN

Jeannie and Ismail stepped into Interpol's San Francisco branch office, a place that held both professional memories and personal history for them. As they entered, Jeannie couldn't help but be flooded with recollections of their previous assignment—tracking down Frank Silva and his notorious former military squad who had been scheming to pilfer the purported Ark of the Covenant.

That case had taken an unexpected turn, leading to a cascade of events that eventually intertwined her life with that of Sean Delaney, the supervising Interpol agent at the time. The mission had ended in disaster but given rise to a love affair that lingered in Jeannie's memories.

The echoes of their footsteps brought her back to the present and, with it, the harsh reality that Sean

Delaney was no longer in this world. His pursuit of the urban terrorist gang known as the Black Cell had ended tragically in a fatal explosion. The weight of his loss and the residual impact of past investigations hung in the air.

"Hey boss, you with me?" Ismail's voice interrupted Jeannie's reverie, drawing her back to the task at hand.

"Huh? Yeah. Sorry. Just remembering the last time we were here," she replied, her tone carrying a mix of nostalgia and solemnity. The office, once a backdrop to triumphs and heartaches, now served as the stage for their renewed commitment to justice as they dived into their current assignment with a sense of purpose and the ghosts of the past never far from their minds.

"Yeah, I know what you mean. I miss 007, too. He was a great guy," Ismail remarked with a hint of nostalgia in his voice. "I wonder if the new director, or whatever they call the branch supervisor at an Interpol office, will have refreshments. Delaney really did a good job at that."

Jeannie chuckled at Ismail's remark. "You just had coffee and donuts at the bureau, and you're already hungry again?"

"Hey, what can I say? When you have a finely tuned body like I have, you must keep providing it with energy," Ismail replied with a mischievous grin.

Jeannie couldn't help but smile at Ismail's lighthearted banter, but a subtle tension lingered beneath the surface. The juxtaposition of humor and the underlying seriousness of their work was a familiar dance, one they had mastered through shared experiences and the unpredictable nature of their roles in the world of international law enforcement. She shook her head, trying to dispel the beginning of another headache that threatened to take hold. "Oh, please, God. Not today," she whispered to herself, silently hoping that the day wouldn't unravel into the kind of chaos they had encountered in the past.

As Jeannie and Ismail entered the Interpol office, they immediately noticed a distinct change in the atmosphere. The familiar office furniture had been replaced with newer pieces and been rearranged since their last visit. The air held the scent of fresh paint and polished surfaces. There was no one to be seen upon their arrival until a tall, lanky, brunette woman entered the room. Her hair was neatly pulled back into a business bun, and she exuded a professional demeanor in her black pantsuit.

"Hello. Can I help you?" she greeted, her voice carrying a refined British accent.

"Yes. I'm Agent Loomis, and this is Agent Flores from the FBI. We have an appointment," Jeannie explained.

"Oh, yes. Mr. Evans is expecting you. Please, follow me," the woman replied, gesturing for them to follow her.

Leading the way through the revamped office space, she guided them to Mr. Evans' office. As they entered, the man in question rose from his desk. Mr. Evans was a towering figure, standing at approximately 6'2". His thin mustache and graying hair added an air of sophistication to his appearance. He extended a welcoming hand after his secretary knocked and introduced Jeannie and Ismail.

"Agents Loomis and Flores, how nice to meet you. Please, have a seat. I'm so glad you could break free from your investigations to assist Interpol," Mr. Evans greeted warmly, motioning toward the chairs arranged in front of his desk. "Would you care for some coffee or tea? I believe we also have some scones."

Before Jeannie could respond, Ismail eagerly chimed in, "That would be great. Coffee for me, and I'd love a scone." Jeannie shot him an evil eye, but he responded with an unapologetic smile.

"Yes, I'd also love some coffee, thank you," Jeannie added, maintaining her composure.

"Florence, could you please get some refreshments for our guests?" Mr. Evans requested. Florence nodded and left the room. "Well, I must say that your reputations precede you, even in the Vatican. The request Interpol received from Rome was quite impressive."

Jeannie leaned forward, her curiosity piqued. "Mr. Evans, I'm sorry, but Agent Flores and I were only told of the Vatican's request and that of Interpol through our supervisor, SAC Lomax, who is just as much in the dark as we are. Could you possibly bring us up to speed?" The anticipation in her voice mirrored the urgency of their mission, and she awaited Mr. Evans' explanation with a focused intensity.

"Oh, quite so. I'm sorry. I just assumed you had already received that background on the case we are investigating," Mr. Evans apologized. The office door reopened, and Florence returned pushing a serving cart laden with coffee, tea, cups, saucers, sugar, and cream. A tempting plate of scones sat in the center.

"Thank you, Florence. Please, agents, help yourselves while I get my file," Mr. Evans suggested. Ismail promptly shot out of his seat, seizing the opportunity to fill a cup with coffee and snatch a scone. Jeannie couldn't help but smile at her partner's eager enthusiasm. The aroma of the freshly brewed coffee prompted Jeannie to anticipate a bout of nausea, so she opted for a bottle of water before returning to her seat.

"I assume you are aware of the recent theft of the Sudarium from a cathedral in Oviedo, Spain?"

"Yes, I have been following the news concerning the theft," Jeannie replied while Ismail eyed another scone on the table. My supervisor did tell us your agency is requesting the FBI to assist in the investigation, but I am still unclear why we were specifically named."

Evans retrieved a letter from the file, laying it on his desk. "Perhaps this will enlighten you."

The letter bore the official Vatican gold letterhead and was signed by Cardinal Kosina. Jeannie quietly read the contents while Ismail seized the opportunity to excuse himself for a second cup of coffee and an additional scone.

"So, what does it say?" Ismail inquired upon his return.

"Well, I'll paraphrase. Apparently, the Vatican received a note addressed to the director of Interpol, who, in turn, received an email suggesting we should be involved in the investigation due to my knowledge of holy relics. The original email implies that the best chance of recovering the Sudarium and returning it to the church lies in our assistance," Jeannie explained.

Turning her attention back to Evans, she asked, "Mr. Evans, do you have a copy of the email sent to the Chief of Interpol?"

He opened the file again and retrieved the printout. "Here you go."

Jeannie, with Ismail looking over her shoulder, scrutinized the email. "Does that email address look strange?" she asked.

"Sure does. It looks like some of the dead-end drops that Darcy and Burk find during a paper chase. When organized crime sets up offshore accounts and communicates, they usually route their emails through multiple servers, making them challenging to trace. This seems similar," Ismail commented, directing his reply to Evans.

"Yeah, but the way it's written also resembles those emails Lomax received when we were chasing down the missing Hitler clone," Jeannie added. "Mr. Evans, is it possible to obtain a copy of your entire case file as well as this?"

"Certainly, I'll get Florence on it right away," Mr. Evans responded, rising and taking the file out to Florence, giving Ismail a chance to help himself to another scone.

"God, I can't take you anywhere, can I?" Jeannie teased Ismail, who remained silent, savoring his snack.

Evans returned with copies of his file and handed them to Jeannie. "Well, frankly, I'm not sure where to start. Perhaps I will gather my team at the bureau and do some brainstorming.

"I'm afraid you won't have much time," Evans said. "You have both been requested to fly to Rome and meet with Cardinal Kosina. They are hoping you can be there in a few days."

CHAPTER SIXTEEN

Seven individuals gathered in a room overlooking the Cathedral of John the Baptist, their attention directed toward the iconic structure. Vincent D'Amico spoke with authority. "That is where our prize is. As you can see, the Cathedral of St. John the Baptist is a relatively simple affair compared to many of Italy's major cathedrals."

He continued, providing a historical context, "Much of the original building suffered damage from a 16th-century fire, leading to extensive restoration efforts. The white brick edifice presents a plain façade adorned with three doors, while a small white dome crowns the entire structure. A square bell tower stands proudly to the right of the main entrance. The Shroud of Turin is now housed in a large, expanded wing situated behind the main altar, and that is where we will strike tomorrow night."

Vincent acknowledged their advantage, "Thanks to Natalia, we now have the information needed for a successful operation. However, as always, be prepared for any unanticipated obstacles that may arise. The Shroud is our target, and our success hinges on precision and adaptability." The group absorbed Vincent's instructions, their focus sharpening on the task that lay ahead within the historical confines of the Cathedral of John the Baptist.

Jeannie and Ismail made their way back to the bureau, returning to the familiar confines of their workplace. Their first order of business was a meeting with SAC Lomax. As they briefed him on the details of their encounter with Mr. Evans and the unfolding investigation, Lomax, in turn, shared a piece of unsettling information he had received during their absence from Washington.

"I don't like this one bit," he expressed, his tone conveying a sense of unease. "I have this gut feeling again that someone is using us as puppets. Your assumption about the anonymous email bouncing around so much that it can't be traced to its source is spot on. Just like the Hitler clone case, someone is pulling the strings behind the scenes, manipulating not just our government but also Interpol and even the Vatican. I'm relieved you two have been requested for this assignment. Cover each other's asses, and that's an order."

The weight of Lomax's words hung in the air as they all grappled with the realization that their involvement in the investigation was not merely because of a straightforward pursuit of justice. The shadows of manipulation and unseen forces loomed over their mission, and Lomax's directive underscored the necessity for vigilance and mutual support within the intricate web of intrigue they found themselves entangled in.

Upon returning home and apprising Delores and her husband of her imminent absence, Jeannie reconvened with Ismail at the bureau. The two were then chauffeured to the airport in preparation for a lengthy flight to Rome. Ismail, ever the master of comfort, convinced Jeannie that indulging in a Cinnabon would be an ideal way to relax during the journey. Succumbing to the allure of the sweet treat, they made a pit stop at a kiosk, acquiring two rolls and two cups of coffee.

Once fortified with their sugary delights, they proceeded to check in their service weapons, a routine yet essential step in their travel protocol. They settled into a brief period of anticipation in the airport's secure environment, the hum of the bustling terminal providing a backdrop as they waited for their plane to arrive. The distant murmur of conversations and the occasional announcement over the intercom contributed to the atmosphere of pre-flight preparations, heightening the sense of impending departure for this crucial assignment in Rome.

"You know, you told me to take a nice long vacation after you blew the wifey and me away with such a generous gift at Christmas. Now look. I'm flying to Rome. Maybe, if we have time, we can visit where the gladiators fought," Ismail remarked.

"You dummy. I meant a non-work-related vacation with your wife and kids. You were supposed to fly to Myrtle Beach, enjoy my beach home, and take in the attractions. Instead, I'm stuck with you for God knows how long."

"Hey, where would the Lone Ranger be without his Tonto? Or Batman without Robin?" Ismail quipped.

"Or Wile E. Coyote without the Roadrunner?" Jeannie replied with a grin. "I'm going to try and take a nap. Wake me when they start serving dinner."

"You got it, boss lady. I'm going to see what movies are on," Ismail said, embracing the camaraderie that defined their partnership as they settled in for the journey.

"Jesus Christ. This place is huge," Ismail exclaimed as he and Jeannie entered Saint Peter's Square, a sprawling plaza located directly in front of St. Peter's Basilica in Vatican City.

"I suggest you don't use that language here, buddy," Jeannie retorted, raising an eyebrow at Ismail's choice of words.

Ismail flashed a sheepish grin. "Well, I guess even the big guy upstairs would be impressed with this setup. Can't blame me for being a little awestruck."

Jeannie chuckled, "Fair enough. Just keep the reverence intact. We're not here on vacation, you know."

"As if I could forget," Ismail quipped. "But hey, a little banter helps lighten the mood. Keeps us on our toes."

"True," Jeannie admitted. "But let's save the irreverence for when we're not standing in the heart of the Vatican. I don't want any lightning bolts striking us down."

Ismail laughed, "Agreed. Lightning bolts and secret missions don't mix well. Now, let's try to find our way around this maze of holy grandeur."

"So, boss, you're the practicing Catholic. Tell me about this place and what I can expect inside. How do I refer to everyone?" Ismail asked seriously while staring at the numerous statutes of saints that surrounded the roof of the square.

"You know, you've got to bring your wife here. You've got the money now. Rome is somewhere everyone should experience at least once. So, we're standing in St. Peter's Square. Look straight ahead, and you've got St. Peter's Basilica, the Pope's official hangout here in Rome."

"That's where the Pope does his thing?" Ismail questioned, finding it a bit challenging to absorb the sheer beauty enveloping them as they strolled.

"And who are all those statues supposed to represent?" Ismail asked while pointing near the roof area.

"Am I your personal tour guide now?" Jeannie teased before addressing his question. "I don't have all 140 names memorized, you know. But sure, there's John the Baptist by Simeon Drouin, Christ the Redeemer by Cristoforo Stati, St. Andrew by Carlo Fancelli, St. John the Evangelist by Antonio Vals, St. James the Great by Giuseppe Fontana, and the list goes on."

"Wow, boss, you've got this down pat. Color me impressed. No wonder they requested you to help on the investigation." Ismail replied, his gaze still fixed on the intricate details of the roofline.

"Now, if we had time, we would head to the right once we step inside, down the seemingly endless hallway, and we'd find ourselves in Michelangelo's Sistine Chapel. I'm really crossing my fingers that we'll have enough time to soak in all the incredible details. Trust me, it's mind-blowing. I visited here with my stepmom in my thirties, and standing beneath that ceiling, realizing Michelangelo painted it while lying on his back for months—mind-blowing."

"Do you think we'll have time?" Ismail inquired.

"Honestly, I've got no clue. We might need to ask for directions once we're in there, especially since I'm not exactly sure where this Cardinal Kosina's office is."

As they stepped into the Basilica, Ismail momentarily froze. The sheer vastness of the interior left him breathless. Jeannie couldn't help but smile, observing her partner and friend attempting to process the overwhelming spectacle, which is no small feat for anyone.

"Good Lord. I've seen this place in movies, but a guy could genuinely get lost in here, even with my stellar investigative skills," Ismail remarked, grinning.

"I'm starting to wonder if the Pope has a psychiatrist on standby for you while we're in Vatican City," Jeannie quipped. They made their way toward an area that seemed to be the starting point for all tours. A priest approached them just before they joined the line.

Father Paul Marino turned to Jeannie and inquired, with a pronounced Italian accent, "Hello, I'm Father Paul Marino. Are you Agents Loomis and Flores?".

"Yes, we are," Jeannie confirmed.

Curious, Ismail questioned, "How did you pick us out in the crowd?"

Without directly answering, Father Marino gestured upward, where both Jeannie and Ismail noticed surveillance cameras. "Interpol sent us your pictures, and facial identification alerted us to your presence. Please follow me. Cardinal Kosina is waiting."

CHAPTER SEVENTEEN

The trio boarded a private elevator and ascended to the second floor. Following Father Marino down yet another corridor, Ismail couldn't help but comment, "This place is like a labyrinth of hallways."

"Tell me about it," Father Marino chuckled. "I've been here for three years, and I still catch myself getting lost now and then. The basement is a whole other story – it's reputed to be a maze I've never dared venture into."

"There's a basement too? What do they stash down there?" Ismail inquired. Jeannie stayed silent, marveling at her partner's relentless curiosity.

"The treasured Tomb of St. Peter is buried under St. Peter's Basilica. It's been an important historical and religious burial site since the 1st century. Built in honor of St. Peter, one of Jesus Christ's twelve apostles, the tomb has several structures that together make up a grand tomb. These structures were created by the Vatican authorities to memorialize the martyrdom of St. Peter," Father Marino answered, apparently pleased to share his knowledge about the cathedral.

"So, you're telling me the real deal, St. Peter's body, is right beneath us?" Ismail asked, clearly taken aback by Father Marino's revelation. Jeannie maintained her smile, enjoying Ismail's astonishment at the unexpected information.

"Yes, St. Peter, formerly known as Simon or Simeon, was one of Christ's twelve disciples and the first leader of the early Christian Church. He led the founding of the Christian Church after Jesus' death, which made him an important figure during the 1st century. St. Peter is considered the first official Pope of Christendom for his contributions to the Church and his role as a leader of the Christian community. Here we are," he knocked on the door before opening it and invited Jeannie and Ismail to enter.

Cardinal Kosina, dressed in traditional scarlet garments, rose to greet his guests from behind a large, highly polished desk and huge leather-bound chair. Jeannie knew the scarlet color represented blood, symbolizing a cardinal's willingness to die for his faith.

"Agents Loomis and Flores. On behalf of the Holy Father, we thank you both for coming to Vatican City to aid us in our investigation of the theft of the

Sudarium." He motioned them to two waiting seats as Father Marino exited the office.

Cardinal Kosina appeared to be well into his late eighties, at least according to Jeannie's estimation. Remnants of white hair peeked out from the sides of his red skull cap, a testament to the passage of time etched on his distinguished countenance. The weight of years seemed to add a certain gravitas to his presence as they approached him.

He extracted a file from his desk yet chose to keep it firmly sealed. "Agent Loomis," he began. "Shortly following the theft of the Sudarium, an anonymous email reached us, emphasizing the urgency of involving you in the investigation. Any idea as to the identity of the individual who strongly recommended your inclusion?"

"No, your Eminence," Agent Loomis responded with a respectful nod. "The FBI has diligently attempted to trace the origins of the email. However, the sender employed a sophisticated network of servers spread across the globe, intentionally obscuring the initial point of origin. It appears to be a meticulously crafted effort to elude detection and maintain anonymity."

Ismail subtly reminded himself to address the Cardinal with the appropriate title, making a mental note to use 'Your Eminence.' Glancing briefly at Jeannie before contributing to the discussion, he began, "Your Eminence, throughout our long flight, Jeannie and I meticulously analyzed the theft from various perspectives. Our conclusions consistently pointed to a critical factor—namely, that the perpetrator or perpetrators must have had access to significant insider information."

Ismail observed Jeannie favor him with a pleased look, clearly impressed by his delivery. Her smile did not go unnoticed, and he felt a sense of satisfaction in her positive reaction.

Cardinal Kosina took a thoughtful pause as if carefully considering his response to Ismail's observations. Eventually, he opened the file on his desk and perused his notes. "You are astute in your assessments. Regrettably, we reached the same conclusion. It appears that the breach in our security emanated from within the cathedral. Someone with intimate knowledge divulged the intricate details of how to circumvent our elaborate security system."

He carefully extracted a photograph from the file and handed it to Jeannie. "Meet Brother Renaldi. Our suspicions rest heavily on him as the likely informant. Despite efforts from both the Spanish police and our Vatican security office, he has proven elusive. It's as if he simply vanished, along with the stolen relic." The Cardinal's expression conveyed a mix of frustration and concern, underlining the severity of the situation.

"Well, I guess that is where we should start," Jeannie said, studying the photograph before passing it to Ismail.

"I sense a need for a change in approach," Cardinal Kosina remarked, his gaze shifting back and forth across his notes. "Today, we received yet another anonymous email. The sender seems to be a few steps ahead of our Vatican security team. According to the message, Brother Renaldi has been located and interrogated. He confessed to providing the valuable information to the thief." Once again, he handed the email to Jeannie, inviting her to read it herself.

As Jeannie started reading the email aloud, the room hushed in anticipation.

"To the esteemed hierarchy of the Holy Catholic Church. You need not further expend your valuable resources in the pursuit of Brother Renaldi. I have located him. He fell victim to blackmail and was coerced into divulging the details of the cathedral's security protecting the Sudarium. He played no direct role in the theft, only providing information. You will not see him again."

The Cardinal's eyes remained fixed on Jeannie, keenly interested in her reaction as she continued reading, "I assume that, by now, your investigative team includes FBI Agents Jeannie Loomis and Ismail Flores. Please provide them with the name 'Vincent.' I understand it's not much, but this person must be a master thief to execute such a daring heist. While concentrating on Vincent, I also suggest investing more effort in uncovering the motivation behind the theft. It's possible he is an art aficionado or acting as a middleman for a buyer. They will figure it out."

The seriousness of the message hung in the air, casting a web of inquiries and potential scenarios for the investigators to navigate. Jeannie passed the email to Ismail, though he displayed minimal interest, recognizing that endeavors to trace and identify the sender resembled a journey into a bottomless rabbit hole. No one spoke for several seconds. Cardinal Kosina rose and opened the door to his office, where a nun pushed in a serving cart with refreshments.

"Let's take a brief respite before delving further. I understand your bodies might still be adjusting to the time change from your flight. Come, let's find repose by the fireplace," Cardinal Kosina suggested, gesturing toward a comfortable seating area.

As they settled, Ismail voiced a question that he'd been pondering in the background, "Father, I mean, your Eminence, we were informed that St. Peter is buried beneath the basilica—his actual body."

The Cardinal nodded in acknowledgment. "Yes, Saint Peter's tomb is a sacred site beneath St. Peter's Basilica, encompassing several graves and a structure erected by Vatican authorities to commemorate the location of Saint Peter's final resting place. Positioned near the west end of a complex of mausoleums known as the Vatican Necropolis, these structures date back to approximately AD 130 to AD 300.

"Visits to the Tomb of Saint Peter and the Necropolis are only permitted with special permission, granted from time to time by the museum. Tradition holds that after St. Peter's death, he was interred on Vatican Hill near the site of his martyrdom. Initially, an ancient basilica was constructed at the location of St. Peter's Tomb, eventually giving way to the current magnificence of St. Peter's Basilica," Cardinal Kosina explained.

"If you wish, before your return to the United States, I can arrange for a comprehensive tour of the Vatican."

"That would be fantastic," Ismail exclaimed, his excitement evident as he glanced at Jeannie, who responded with a smiling nod.

"Cardinal Kovina," Jeannie began thoughtfully, "as the anonymous email suggests, perhaps our focus should extend beyond Vincent. We should delve into potential motives behind the theft," she added, taking a sip of her tea, her gaze lingering on the Cardinal in anticipation of his response.

"The Church entertains two plausible scenarios," Cardinal Kovina began, choosing his words with care. "The first, as the email writer alluded to, is that a singular thief or a group of thieves targeted the relic either for personal gain or with the intention to sell it to a collector." He paused. A moment of uncertainty hung in the room, acknowledged by both Jeannie and Ismail, who exchanged a fleeting glance.

"And the other possibility?" Jeannie inquired, her curiosity urging the Cardinal to share more.

Cardinal Kovina hesitated, grappling with the delicate nature of his revelations. "The other, more disquieting, possibility involves a schism within the Church itself. There's an internal struggle, a rift, and it pains me to say that traditionalists within our ranks may have played a role in this theft."

The weight of his revelation settled over the room, leaving an air of tension as the investigators absorbed the unexpected disclosure about a potential conflict within the Church.

CHAPTER EIGHTEEN

"I'm sorry, I don't follow," Ismail admitted, seeking clarification. "What schism are you referring to?"

Jeannie was poised to respond, but Cardinal Kovina preempted her. "Agent Flores, the Church has experienced a transformation of sorts, stemming from the contrasting beliefs of our current Pope Francis and the late Pope John Paul II, now Saint John Paul. Pope John Paul was a staunch traditionalist, his belief firmly anchored in biblical doctrines, while Pope Francis, hailing from a socialist background, embraces a more liberal perspective. This ideological dichotomy has resulted in a rift within the Church, akin to the divisions seen in your country."

The Cardinal's words unveiled a nuanced struggle within the Catholic Church, where the clash of conservative and liberal ideologies mirrored broader societal challenges. The investigators absorbed this insight, realizing that the theft of the Sudarium might be entwined with the turbulence caused by these ideological differences within the Church itself.

"So, what are you alluding to?" Jeannie inquired, her gaze fixed on Cardinal Kovina. "Are you suggesting that individuals within the hierarchy of the Catholic Church might be responsible for the theft of the Sudarium? And if so, what purpose could they possibly have in mind?"

Cardinal Kovina met her probing gaze, cognizant of the significance of the implications. "Agent Loomis, it's a distressing possibility but one we cannot dismiss outright. The schism within the Church, exacerbated by differing ideologies, has led to factions with varying degrees of allegiance to tradition and reform. Some individuals, disillusioned or motivated by their beliefs, may perceive the Sudarium as a symbol to be used for their cause. Whether it's to oppose the Church's current direction, to assert a particular interpretation of its doctrines, or for personal gain, the motives could be complex and multifaceted."

As he spoke, the weight of the situation hung heavily in the room, leaving the investigators grappling with the unsettling notion that the perpetrators might be found within the very institution they were tasked with protecting and serving.

Jeannie and Ismail regrouped in the hotel restaurant after returning to their rooms. "I reached out to both Lomax and Darcy, providing them with the updates from our conversation with Cardinal Kovina," Jeannie shared. "Darcy seems determined and ready to take on the task of locating this supposed master thief, assuming he even exists. What are your thoughts on the motives Cardinal Kovina suggested the Church might be grappling with?" she inquired, perusing the menu as she posed the question.

"Well, much like you, I can envision a skilled suspect or a group driven by the direct desire to steal the relic, possibly for personal gain or to hand it over to an art collector for a substantial sum. However, I believe the other potential motive warrants consideration, especially by someone who attends church regularly like you do. It's something I'm now contemplating after my experience inside the Vatican."

"Oh, my God. You're going to start going to church now. Just give me a heads-up, so if it happens to be the same church that I'm in, I can make a swift exit in case the roof decides to collapse when you walk in."

"Funny. Very funny. Aren't you supposed to be encouraging me?" they bantered, sharing a laugh before placing their order.

As they savored the delectable Italian cuisine, the two couldn't help but comment on the exquisite flavors of the dishes. Later, seated over cups of coffee, Jeannie delved into a more profound conversation, elaborating on Cardinal Kovina's insights regarding the schism within the Church.

"There's a significant truth in what Cardinal Kovina mentioned about the potential motive involving traditional and liberal Catholics," Jeannie remarked thoughtfully. "The present divisions within the Church have deep political roots, mirroring a profound rift between Pope Francis and predominantly Western Catholics. It's a complex interplay of ideologies, and the tension has created a conspicuous divide within the Church's global community."

"What do you think about the new Pope?" Ismail inquired.

"I have to admit, I'm not a fan," Jeannie replied. "I thought his selection was a mistake. He aligns with a progressive socialist ideology, and I was concerned that he might try to inject that into a Church that thrived under the leadership of Pope John Paul II. The two camps have, respectively, shown a particular devotion for one of the two previous popes, John Paul II and Benedict XVI, or for the present one, Francis. One reputed arch-conservative, Cardinal Raymond Burke, I believe his name is, has warned that Francis will split the Church community with his ideas and policies."

"At first glance, it's challenging to appreciate why there's such a fuss. The schism started when the new Pope told parishes they could no longer hold Mass in Latin unless they received permission from their bishops. However, Latin Mass enthusiasts constitute a small minority of practicing Catholics, and most Church traditionalists—whether bishops, priests, or laypeople—are content to participate in Masses conducted in their everyday language," Jeannie explained.

"The discontent arises from various factors, including a decline in Catholics' engagement with Mass, concerns about the quality of the liturgy, frustrations over what's perceived as a progressive direction in Pope Francis's pontificate, and lingering dissatisfaction with Vatican II. Traditionalists view the council not as a thorough reform but as something between a modest course correction and a betrayal of the Church's patrimony," she continued, sensing Ismail's potential confusion.

"Now, you're starting to go over my head with all this Vatican II and patrimony talk," Ismail replied. "But let's assume, for argument's sake, that a group of priests are upset with the Church. What good does stealing the Sudarium do for their cause?"

"To me, that is the missing piece. This anonymous email writer is on the right trail, I think. If we can discover the motive, we will be on the fast track to catching the suspect or suspects and retrieving the relic. Let's get some sleep. Hopefully, Darcy and Burk will come up with something tomorrow."

CHAPTER NINETEEN

As Jeannie awoke and powered up her laptop, she discovered a cluster of emails waiting for her—some from Darcy, others from Burk. Among the messages were articles featuring Vincent D'Amico. Described as an entrepreneur, Jeannie's instincts whispered a different narrative, painting him as a ruthless businessman likely rooted in old money. The accompanying images reinforced this impression, portraying him as a charismatic playboy surrounded by an entourage of stunning women. One with long raven hair added an air of sophistication to the scenes.

Before delving further into her reading material, a relentless, pounding headache resurged. Hastily, she reached for the medication prescribed by Dr. Goldsmith, her memory failing to confirm whether she had already taken it earlier. Returning to her bed, she lay back, soothing her forehead with a chilled washcloth. The room appeared to spin around her. She looked at her phone for the time, endeavoring to calculate the time difference between Rome and San Francisco to call her doctor.

While waiting for her headache to subside, she computed a nine-hour time gap. Given that it was 5:53 a.m. in her hotel room, Dr. Goldsmith's office should still be open, being 2:53 p.m. in that time zone. She gradually stood up from her bed, placing the washcloth on a nightstand, and dialed the doctor's office.

"Hello, Dr. Goldsmith's office. Can I help you?" came a pleasant female greeting.

After Jeannie identified herself, she was put on a short pause to listen to what Ismail called, 'elevator music.'

Dr. Goldsmith's reassuring voice came through the phone. Jeannie hesitated for a moment, then gathered the courage to ask about her biopsy results. In a calm yet serious tone, Dr. Goldsmith conveyed the news: "Jeannie, I'm afraid the biopsy indicates that you have gliosarcoma."

He went on to explain the nature of the diagnosis, detailing the characteristics of gliosarcoma and what it meant for her health. Despite the shock, Jeannie listened intently, absorbing the information that would reshape her understanding of the challenges ahead. Dr. Goldsmith assured her that they would discuss potential treatment options and create a plan to navigate this difficult journey together.

"Dr. Goldsmith, I implore you not to sugarcoat anything. The mere name gliosarcoma is ominous enough," she pleaded.

Dr. Goldsmith hesitated, his usual preference for delivering such news in a more supportive environment evident in his contemplative pause. "Jeannie, typically, I prefer to discuss these matters in person within the comforting confines of my office and ideally with the presence of a relative or close friend for support."

Understanding the situation and the challenges posed by her current circumstances, Jeannie interrupted, "I understand, Doctor, but given my current official business in Italy, that's just not possible right now. So, if you could, please be straightforward with me."

The request hung in the air, a palpable tension building as both parties anticipated the weight of the conversation about to unfold.

"I regret to inform you that gliosarcoma is currently incurable. Our treatment approach aims to manage and restrict the tumor's growth for as long as feasible. Typically, surgery to extract the tumor is the initial step, but due to the infiltration of healthy brain tissue, complete removal of all cancerous cells is often impossible," Dr. Goldsmith explained solemnly.

Processing this heavy information, Jeannie asked, her voice strained with emotion, "How long can someone live with gliosarcoma?" Tears traced paths down her cheeks.

Dr. Goldsmith answered compassionately, "This high-grade malignant tumor carries a grim prognosis. The average survival time ranges from four to 18 months. However, it is exceptionally rare for it to exceed four months." His sympathetic tone aimed to soften the harsh reality of the prognosis, acknowledging the difficulty of the news he had just delivered.

"What signs should I be on the lookout for as the cancer progresses?" Jeannie inquired, her voice steady despite the weight of the conversation.

"Hallucinations and, in some cases, psychosis. Loss of appetite, bouts of nausea, and, of course, worsening headaches," Dr. Goldsmith responded, a somber pause lingering in the air before Jeannie pressed on with her questions.

"How will I know I'm approaching the end of life?" she asked, her voice betraying the difficulty of the question.

"In the final weeks, you may experience drowsiness or loss of consciousness. Lethargy, confusion, and a reversal of night and day may occur. Unfortunately, these symptoms are common and tend to intensify in the last week of life. I'm truly sorry, Jeannie," Dr. Goldsmith expressed, his tone reflecting both empathy and the stark reality of the situation.

"Well… I guess a hospice is in my future." Dr. Goldsmith did not immediately answer. Finally, after clearing his throat, he asked Jeannie to make an appointment with him as soon as she returned to the States.

Overwhelmed by the devastating news of her tragic prognosis, Jeannie found herself grappling with a complex mix of emotions. The weight of her diagnosis pressed upon her as she contemplated the decision to share this distressing information with loved ones. The urgency of taking care of her affairs and tying up loose ends loomed large in her thoughts, intertwining with the pressing need to conclude her investigation into the theft of the Sudarium.

Despite the turmoil within her, Jeannie's determination shone through as she grappled with the delicate balance between confronting the harsh reality of her failing health and ensuring the completion of her professional commitments. In the face of adversity, she remained resolute, seeking to navigate both personal and professional spheres with grace and purpose.

She encountered Ismail in the hotel dining room, though her lack of appetite led her to settle for a simple cup of tea. "Something wrong, boss?" Ismail inquired, busying himself with his breakfast.

She took a moment before responding, her thoughts anchored in the information Burk and Darcy had gathered. "No, just pondering the details they've unearthed for us. My gut instinct strongly suggests that Vincent D'Amico is somehow linked to the theft. He's not only an art connoisseur but also possesses substantial wealth, appearing to be a thrill-seeker at heart," she explained, a sense of determination underlining her words. As Ismail continued devouring his breakfast, she couldn't shake the feeling that the key to solving the mystery lay in untangling the enigma surrounding D'Amico's involvement.

D'Amico gathered his team for a final briefing in the heart of Turin, Italy. "In just a few minutes, we'll make our move on the church. We're all familiar with the layout," he began, his instructions firm. "Tim, disable the alarm systems. Rafael, Thomas, get the Shroud ready for extraction. It's likely that Ruben and Samuel will also be needed to lift the relic. Natalia, as usual, hang back in case any unexpected obstacles arise."

Natalia, her suppressed firearm in hand, affirmed her readiness. "I'm prepared for any obstacles that come our way."

"Now, once we secure the Shroud, we backtrack to the waiting van where Miguel will be stationed. I'll provide the address for our destination. This part is a bit tricky. We lack intel on where the priests will meet us. We'll showcase the relic, but it stays in the van. After they make the payment, Natalia and I will handle them. Then, we take a leisurely drive back to the castle. Alright, let's move out," D'Amico concluded, their illicit operation hanging in the air as the team prepared to execute their carefully laid plan.

CHAPTER TWENTY

Jeannie and Ismail secured a flight to Oviedo, Spain, and after hailing a cab, arrived at Vincent D'Amico's medieval-style castle. "Damn, you're right. This guy must have some bucks. Look at the scale of this. It's like we've gone back to the Middle Ages. I would not be surprised to find knights covered in armor rushing out of the castle over the manmade moat, waving their swords," Ismail said, taking in the sight.

When they arrived at what they thought was the front gate, they pulled on a rope that rang a bell on top of the wall. Ismail pulled the rope several times, but no one came to the gate. "Huh. Guess no one is at home," Ismail said.

Jeannie motioned to two sets of surveillance cameras that showed their presence. "Well, whether they are home or not, they know we are here." They walked back to the waiting cab and left. While riding in the van, D'Amico received an alert that someone was at the castle gate. He enlarged the video showing Jeannie and Ismail and then handed his phone to Tim.

"If possible, use your facial recognition software and see if you can identify these two individuals. I suspect they are law enforcement."

Upon arrival outside the Cathedral of Turin, the scene perfectly mirrored the images D'Amico had displayed in his briefing slides. "Remember, once we breach the cathedral, our destination is the chapel in the back. That's where the Shroud is kept," he reminded the team.

Miguel skillfully maneuvered the van into the shadows, expertly parking it for their covert operation. D'Amico led the way after exiting the van, followed by Natalia. As the team gathered in front of the main door, Natalia deftly neutralized the locking mechanism, and the door creaked open, revealing the enveloping aroma of candles and incense. The church was still aglow with numerous lit candles, rendering flashlights unnecessary.

Navigating the candlelit interior, the team made their way to the chapel. Vincent pointed to a picture on the wall, and Tim promptly removed it, revealing a large display panel. Extracting a schematic diagram from his pocket, Tim placed a penlight between his teeth. Studying the diagram and the corresponding panel, he carefully manipulated several wires, causing the panel to illuminate with a green light. Tim glanced at Vincent, nodding in confirmation.

With the panel now activated, the team cautiously entered the chapel, but Natalia remained outside, vigilant and scanning for any potential intruders that might pose a threat to their operation. The air inside was thick with tension and the scent of religious devotion as the team advanced toward their objective, aware that the success of their mission hinged on a delicate balance of precision and stealth.

"It's not here," sighed Rafael, sounding disappointed as he gazed at the vast empty table mirroring the dimensions of the Shroud.

"Take it easy, my dear friend. Remember, as I explained in my briefings, seeing the authentic Shroud of Turin isn't actually feasible. However, replicas and exhibits in the nearby museum effectively convey the Shroud's significance and unravel its mysteries. Artifacts linked to the Holy Shroud are on display, accompanied by information detailing its intricate history and the numerous studies conducted on it. But the actual relic is housed in this concealed space," he gestured toward a section of the wall, deftly turning a hidden handle. The door opened, unveiling an interior room.

"Our treasure lies within this climate-controlled enclosure in this specially constructed chapel. Due to its exceptionally fragile condition, the shroud remains hidden from public view except during rare exhibitions. Again, if you remember my briefing, the last public display occurred in 2015, drawing millions of visitors. There are presently no immediate plans for future exhibitions. While people journey to Turin to explore and honor the Shroud, they are denied direct visual access to the relic. However, my friends, now, you are in for a treat—behold the glory of the Shroud in all its splendor."

The group stood in a circle, transfixed by the sight of the Shroud, their focus fixed on studying its features. An unbroken hush enveloped them; no words were exchanged. Without guidance, the group quietly navigated around the relic, each member deep in contemplation. Thomas was the first to break the silence.

"Looks heavy with all those layers of glass."

"Yes, and not just any glass, but bulletproof. Alright, let's stop staring and transport it to the van," D'Amico commanded. The group, except for Natalia, exerted themselves to lift the container, retracing their steps. They had to pause, catching their breath and gathering strength before pressing on twice during their journey. Finally, they arrived at the van. After several attempts, they managed to carefully place the treasure on a thick layer of foam rubber to provide a protective cushion. With the task accomplished, they all climbed into the van, ready to depart. The weight of the secured artifact lingered in the air as they settled in for the journey ahead.

Upon returning to their hotel, Jeannie informed Ismail of an impending headache and decided to retire for some much-needed rest. "What did your doctor say?" Ismail inquired as she made her way out of the lobby.

"He prescribed new pills, but they tend to make me drowsy. Why don't you go explore the city? I'll text you once I feel better," she suggested.

As Jeannie stepped away, she grappled with the burden of keeping her profound diagnosis hidden, recognizing that Ismail and his crew were more than just friends—they were her chosen family. Thoughts raced through her mind as she considered the practicalities that lay ahead. Updating her will and trust became a pressing task, with a significant portion earmarked for Ismail and his loved ones. She also would allocate a sum to her dedicated housekeeper, who was entrusted with the care of her mansion in Myrtle Beach and her mother's aging cat.

Her contemplation extended to her ever-watchful neighbors, Walter and Delores. Despite their busybody tendencies, their loyalty deserved acknowledgment in her final arrangements. Even her oblivious boss, Lomax, lingered in her thoughts, unaware of her inheritance. Lost in this whirlwind of considerations, Jeannie succumbed to sleep, her subconscious navigating the delicate details of what lay ahead.

CHAPTER TWENTY-ONE

As night descended over Spain, Delaney, clad entirely in black, including a knit cap and leather gloves, skillfully utilized the cloak of darkness to mask his approach to Vincent D'Amico's castle. Armed with a flashlight that he used sparingly, he cautiously advanced toward the imposing structure, taking note of its moat and gate. The glint of surveillance cameras caught his attention, prompting a strategic retreat. Rather than assaulting the front, he redirected his approach to the side façade.

He aimed his grappling gun toward the summit of the castle wall. The metallic clink echoed as the grappling hook seemingly secured onto something substantial, allowing Delaney to initiate his ascent. Scaling the heights, he paused at the top to listen for any signs of occupants within. Detecting only silence, he carefully maneuvered over the wall. The meticulous detail and craftsmanship invested in the castle's construction surprised him as he surveyed his surroundings in the moonlight. The air was thick with anticipation as he ventured deeper into the heart of the fortress, his senses heightened and his mission unfolding in the shadows.

Before descending to ground level, he removed the grappling hook and retrieved his climbing rope. He performed a comprehensive 360-degree survey of the castle, employing infrared lenses for heightened visibility. No traces of body warmth were detected; the castle stood in solitude. He found himself in complete isolation.

Drawn toward what seemed to be the central structure, he advanced and discovered that, curiously, the front door was unlocked. Without hesitation, he entered the dimly lit interior. As anticipated, the space was adorned with numerous displays featuring knights in shining armor, their stoic figures standing sentinel-like. The walls boasted an array of coats of arms, their intricate designs hinting at a storied past, though he couldn't ascertain their connection to D'Amico.

According to the intelligence gathered by Delaney's organization, Vincent D'Amico was a grade-A narcissist, perpetually dissatisfied with his acquisitions. The echo of a James Bond movie, *Thunderball*, resonated in his mind, drawing a parallel with that villain who was driven by insatiable desires. It became evident that D'Amico shared this trait: an incessant craving for more, a characteristic that heightened the complexity of the mission at hand. Delaney, surrounded by the silent guardians of armor-clad knights, felt the weight of the challenge ahead in this enigmatic fortress.

Delaney located what seemed to be D'Amico's office, a space adorned with the most expansive saltwater aquarium he had ever encountered outside of a museum. The thickness of the glass seemed to amplify the presence of the marine life within. Majestic sharks, graceful rays, and an array of vibrant fish coexisted in a mesmerizing aquatic ballet within the confines of the colossal tank.

Even with the knowledge that the castle was vacant, he used his flashlight rather than turn on any lights. He found what he was looking for among the scattered documents on D'Amico's desk: a diagram of the interior of the Cathedral of San Salvador, Oviedo, Spain, along with a printout of what appeared to be a panel for a security alarm. Bingo, he thought. He continued his search but found nothing more.

As he marveled at the captivating marine life within the aquarium, a subtle anomaly in his peripheral vision caught his attention —a lever discreetly positioned near the vast library. Intrigued, he flipped the lever, unveiling a concealed door that smoothly opened, revealing a spiral staircase. Delaney couldn't help but acknowledge the clichéd but appropriate nature of discovering hidden doors and passageways in a medieval castle.

"Naturally. I'm in a medieval castle, so hidden doors and passageways are par for the course," he mused silently, allowing a wry smile to cross his face. With a deliberate step, he commenced his descent down the spiral staircase, the hidden depths of the castle awaiting him like a mysterious abyss.

Descending halfway, it dawned on him that he was stepping into a meticulously crafted reproduction of a medieval dungeon. The ambiance exuded an eerie authenticity, complete with cages for torture and vacant cells. While the implements of torment and incarceration appeared to be mere decorative elements, doubt lingered in his mind. The line between historical representation and functional reality blurred, leaving him unable to definitively dismiss the possibility that, despite their apparent emptiness, these cages and cells might hold more than just a decorative purpose.

He noticed another room adjacent to the primary chamber beckoning for exploration. Feeling secure in the depths of the structure, he decided to illuminate the space. As the lights flickered to life, he found himself momentarily stunned. The Sudarium lay within a specially designed containment area and was prominently displayed. The discovery gripped him, and he couldn't help but marvel at the significance of the relic now within his view.

He slowly approached, looking out for any booby traps that D'Amico may have put in place. Finding none, he stood over the relic. Not being a religious person, Delaney still marveled at the Shroud of Oviedo, a bloodstained piece of cloth measuring 33 x 21 inches. He knew the Sudarium was thought to be the cloth that was wrapped around Jesus Christ's head. He continued to study the piece through its protective glass.

The Sudarium exhibited clear indications of advanced deterioration, marked by dark flecks symmetrically arranged throughout its surface. Unlike the Shroud of Turin, whose markings formed discernible images, the Sudarium's features remained elusive.

He entered a second room that was much larger than the one he was in. Equally startled, he came face to face with the Shroud of Turin. He approached slowly, again looking for booby traps

The silence was abruptly shattered by the unexpected vibration of his cell phone, interrupting his intense exploration and causing a momentary startle. Glancing at the screen, the Caller ID displayed nothing. "Must be headquarters," he surmised with a confident guess. His intuition proved correct.

"Delaney. Where are you?" the voice on the other end demanded, devoid of any formal greeting.

"Sir, I'm inside D'Amico's castle," Delaney responded.

"Well, finish up there. The Shroud of Turin has just been stolen."

A moment of confusion gripped Delaney as he processed the shocking information. "Sir, I'm standing in a room where the Shroud of Turin is displayed," he interjected.

"What? What's that you say? Delaney, that is impossible. The theft of the Shroud of Turin was just discovered; how in the hell could it be in Spain? Get to it and report back as soon as you have anything," the urgency in his supervisor's voice mirrored the perplexity Delaney felt. As the weight of the situation sunk in, Delaney's focus shifted from the Sudarium to the unfolding mystery of the missing Shroud of Turin. The room's atmosphere grew tense as he grappled with the implications of this unexpected turn of events.

He immersed himself in a meticulous examination of the Shroud of Turin, fully aware that his expertise fell short of that of an art critic. Nevertheless, he possessed some knowledge about the Shroud, and as he focused on the facial area of the cloth, a disconcerting familiarity struck him.

The resemblance was uncanny, echoing the images he had seen before. Moving to other sections of the Shroud only intensified the impression that this could, indeed, be the authentic article. The question gnawed at him — how was this possible?

Returning to D'Amico's office, he intensified his search, delving deeper into the desk and drawers. His mind raced, hoping that dredging up his recollections might unveil clues about how the Shroud could exist in two seemingly disparate locations. "Think, Delaney. Think."

The enigma deepened as he contemplated the mysterious creation of the Shroud's image. Scientific studies had grappled with the elusive nature of the image, portraying a man believed to be Jesus Christ. The faint, brownish color and negative appearance sparked speculation about the mechanism behind its formation. Theories abounded, from natural processes involving bodily fluids to artistic or chemical methods. Yet, conclusive evidence remained elusive, leaving the origins of the image cloaked in ambiguity.

In his pursuit of answers, Delaney discovered a crucial revelation within a folder. Correspondence with various individuals revealed discussions surrounding the utilization of artificial intelligence enhanced to replicate a near-identical Shroud of Turin. This advanced copy was crafted with such precision that only upon close examination could one discern its artificial nature, making it a deceptive duplicate of the revered relic. The realization sent a chill down Delaney's spine, unraveling a web of intrigue that stretched far beyond the confines of D'Amico's castle.

Back in the chamber cradling the Sudarium, Delaney couldn't shake the disconcerting feeling that this relic appeared eerily authentic. The room housing the Shroud of Turin, now suspected to be counterfeit, stirred a growing suspicion within him that the Shroud might be the product of artificial intelligence—a meticulously crafted imitation designed to deceive even the most discerning eye. But the looming question persisted: Why? If D'Amico had successfully pilfered the genuine Shroud, what purpose could a counterfeit serve?

This newfound revelation opened a labyrinth of possibilities, prompting Delaney to reconsider the motives at play. Was the duplicate Shroud part of a larger scheme, a ploy to divert attention or perhaps safeguard the genuine artifact? The complexity of the situation deepened, leading him to question not only the authenticity of the relics but also the intricate web of intentions woven by those involved.

CHAPTER TWENTY-TWO

As he stood in the enigmatic chamber, Delaney grappled with the realization that the answers he sought extended far beyond the confines of mere theft. The Shroud, whether real or artificial, had become a pivotal piece in a puzzle that seemed to transcend the boundaries of conventional crime.

Glancing at his watch, Delaney concluded that he had dedicated ample time to exploring the castle's mysteries. Before exiting, a strategic move occurred to him. In a calculated act, he discreetly affixed a tracking device to both the Sudarium and the Shroud, ensuring a digital tether that would guide his investigation moving forward. Following this subtle yet crucial act, he retraced his earlier steps, seamlessly blending into the shadows once more.

As he ventured back into the enveloping darkness, Delaney harbored a sense of anticipation. The tracking devices, now silently transmitting their signals, transformed the relics into breadcrumbs, leading him through the labyrinthine complexities of the unfolding mystery. The castle, with its secrets and enigmas, seemed to pulse with heightened energy as he navigated the obscure passages, each step propelling him deeper into the heart of the unfolding intrigue.

Jeannie's slumber was abruptly interrupted by the insistent ring of her cell phone. The caller ID revealed Ismail's name, and as she fumbled to grab the device, her groggy gaze flickered to her watch. The time eluded her as her bleary eyes failed to focus on the numbers.

"What's up, Ace?" she mumbled, her voice still carrying the remnants of sleep.

"You going to sleep the day away?" Ismail's teasing voice greeted her. "I already ran with the bulls and got hit on by several señoritas."

"In your dreams. Where are you?" Jeannie inquired, attempting to shake off her grogginess.

"I'm ready to grab some lunch. Interested?" Ismail suggested.

"Yeah. I'll be right down," Jeannie responded, gingerly rising from the bed. A glance at the clock hinted that some time had passed, and she noticed her headache had subsided somewhat. An underlying concern lingered as she contemplated the inevitable onset of symptoms she would face. "I wonder how long I can continue eating without vomiting," she mused to herself, aware that the day ahead might be a delicate balance between enjoyment and the impending challenges her body would present.

Her cell went off again before she could exit the elevator to the lobby area. She did not recognize the number. "Loomis," she answered.

"Agent Loomis, this is Cardinal Kovina. Add the theft of the Shroud of Turin to your investigation."

Once again, the hallowed ambiance of the La Pergo Restaurant dining room played host to esteemed guests Cardinal Rodger McCormick, Cardinal Agostino Vallini, and Cardinal Francis Mahoney. Cardinal Mahoney broke the thoughtful silence that enveloped the trio. "The Shroud has been successfully acquired. However, due to its considerable size, our procurer insists on a personal exchange and has chosen a location suitable for the transfer."

Cardinal Vallini inquired, "And where do you propose this exchange takes place?"

"I've secured a modest room, already outfitted with the necessary environmental controls to ensure the Shroud's safekeeping. The owner, a devout believer, considers it an honor to assist us in this sacred endeavor to establish the New Church," Cardinal Mahoney assured.

Seizing the moment, Cardinal McCormick shifted the discussion toward another crucial artifact. "This meeting might be an opportune time to address the acquisition of the final relic—the True Cross. Have we reached a consensus on the payment we are willing to offer?"

Cardinals Vallini and Mahoney nodded in unison. "Excellent," Cardinal McCormick continued. "In the past week, I've maintained communication with Cardinals and Bishops in the United States, keeping them abreast of our progress in securing all three relics. The response from America has been overwhelmingly positive, with a robust enthusiasm for the establishment of the New Catholic Church.

"I feel the main stumbling block between the United States and Europe will be the proposed new location for what I call Vatican City II," Cardinal McCormick said. "The proposed venue for Vatican City II could emerge as a primary hurdle in fostering collaboration between the United States and Europe." He expanded on his viewpoint, acknowledging the complexities inherent in determining a location that would be acceptable to both regions. "The divergent perspectives and cultural nuances between the two continents make finding common ground for this significant endeavor particularly challenging."

Elaborating on the intricacies of the matter, Cardinal McCormick emphasized the need for thoughtful consideration and diplomatic navigation. "The geopolitical and symbolic significance of the chosen site cannot be underestimated. It must resonate with the spiritual and historical ethos of both the American and European Catholic communities, fostering a sense of shared purpose and identity."

Cardinal McCormick referred to the necessity for open dialogue and compromise while contemplating the way forward. "To overcome this potential stumbling block, it is imperative that we engage in earnest discussions, seeking input from representatives on both sides of the Atlantic. A collaborative decision-making process will ensure that the new Vatican City II becomes a unifying force rather than a divisive factor in our collective pursuit of a renewed and strengthened Catholic Church."

"I've got a bit of Shroud knowledge up my sleeve," Ismail remarked with a knowing smile after Jeannie shared her conversation with Cardinal Kovina. "The radiation imprint on the Shroud is something of a technological marvel. It's a three-dimensional layered spectrum that surpasses the capabilities of our most advanced tools—lasers and supercomputers included. There's simply nothing comparable on Earth."

Jeannie responded with a playful grin, "Wow, aren't you a walking Wikipedia? Please, professor, enlighten us further."

Ismail chuckled before continuing, "Well, I do watch the History Channel. I'm not all about sports and bathing suit competitions. Now, the blood on the Shroud is quite fascinating. It's of the rare AB negative type, yet there's a peculiar absence of the

Y chromosome, indicating a sole maternal origin. Further analyses have revealed traces of extreme suffering, with heightened bilirubin levels and minute particles of sand near the ankle and injured knee bearing a distinct mineral combination exclusive to the path of Golgotha. And let's not forget the pollen particles native to Jerusalem, specifically produced in March-April, adorning the fabric."

Jeannie playfully interjected, "Gee, you should retire from the bureau and become an art professor. I bet people would beat down the door to get into your classroom."

Ismail grinned, "Please, I'm on a roll here. The specter on the cloth defies conventional expectations. It suggests the body's ethereal suspension radiating from within without external pressure. Examinations even detected particles of vinegar near the mouth and beard area. The power source itself exhibits X-ray properties, revealing three-dimensional spectra in areas like the hands, the phalanges of inner finger bones, and the teeth under the lower lip. The blood defied clotting due to a substance released by the body under extreme pain, and, remarkably, it continues to bleed after death."

Jeannie remarked with a thoughtful expression, "He still bleeds after his death."

"Indeed," Ismail agreed before pressing on. "The lateral incision on the victim's side released blood and water from his lung, its dimensions aligning precisely with the spearhead used by the Roman army in the 1st century. Double parallel engravings, reminiscent of the Roman whips with metal spheres at the ends, adorned the back of his arms and thighs. Similar blood, seeds, and facial marks surfaced in the Sudarium of Oviedo in Spain."

Jeannie, realizing Ismail was now a believer, asked, "So, you and I believe the same person was covered with the facial cloth and has their image on the Shroud?"

"Exactly," Ismail confirmed. "It's like a napkin, and recent revelations suggest the Shroud isn't a funeral cloth but a tablecloth, possibly hurriedly acquired for Jesus' burial. Traditionally, in Israel, a person's blood is buried with them. Even today, when a soldier or civilian falls, the cloth is interred with the body."

Jeannie added, "Well, my new believer, The Gospel of John hinted at the cloth covering Jesus's head being folded and laid aside in the stone tomb. Recent findings disclose that the carbon-dated sample originated from a corner of the Turin Shroud, repaired with intertwined cotton threads around 1400 AD."

Ismail, caught up in the narrative, mused, "Hey, I think we really nailed it with this whole Sudarium and Shroud connection. It's like we've got this puzzle figured out. The only hiccup is, well, we're still missing Jesus' DNA to wrap it all up."

CHAPTER TWENTY-THREE

Jeannie and Ismail swiftly arranged a flight to Turin, fueled by the urgency to interview anyone possessing insights into the recent theft. The duo couldn't shake the feeling that they were a few steps behind both the Vatican security detail and the elusive anonymous emailer who seemed to be orchestrating this intricate puzzle.

Mid-flight, backed by the hum of the aircraft, Jeannie turned to Ismail, her eyes reflecting both determination and curiosity, and asked, "Have you given any more thought to the emailer?".

Ismail glanced out of the window for a moment before turning his attention back to Jeannie. He nodded, "Yeah. It sure seems reminiscent of those anonymous emails that played a crucial role in guiding us through the Hitler clone case. Let's call this mysterious figure the Phantom. It appears the Phantom is operating with an uncanny proximity to the unfolding events, much closer than we currently find ourselves."

As the plane cruised above the clouds, the duo delved into speculation about the Phantom's motives and connection to the unfolding events. The intrigue of the situation added a layer of suspense to their investigation. It was a race against time, and they were determined to bridge the gap and catch up with the elusive figure who seemed to be pulling the strings from the shadows.

Turin's atmosphere buzzed with both history and mystery. Jeannie and Ismail wasted no time in initiating interviews with individuals who might possess critical information. The air was thick with anticipation as they sought to unravel the layers of the Shroud's theft and the enigmatic presence of the Phantom. Each conversation brought them closer to the heart of the matter, yet their adversary's elusive nature kept them on their toes.

The investigation in Turin unfolded like a complex chess game, with moves and countermoves propelling Jeannie and Ismail deeper into an unknown labyrinth. The Phantom's influence seemed to be a constant, an unseen force shaping the narrative. As the agents combed through clues and testimonies, they couldn't escape the feeling that the Phantom was orchestrating a carefully calculated dance, leaving breadcrumbs for them to follow.

Once more, Jeannie and Ismail found themselves in accord, sharing the conviction that the success of such a dynamic heist necessitated insider information. It was apparent that someone with intimate knowledge of the Vatican's security measures and the layout of the premises had played a crucial role in orchestrating the theft. The sheer scale and intricacies of the operation suggested an inside connection, providing the thieves with a significant advantage.

In a further twist, the individual who unquestionably provided the insider information had met a tragic end. A case of suicide, according to the Italian police. Jeannie and Ismail promptly found themselves at odds with the official narrative when they arrived at the site of this mysterious death. Their skepticism arose from the observation that the stool, believed to be how the victim reached the fatal noose, seemed insufficient for the task. Rather than divulging their differing perspective to the authorities, they chose to redirect their focus to a grander puzzle—the elusive whereabouts of the Shroud of Turin.

The Shroud's sheer size added to the complexity of the situation. Jeannie elaborated, "The relic is no petite item. It measures 14 feet 3 inches long and 3 feet 7 inches wide. Couple that with the layers of bulletproof glass, akin to what encased the Sudarium, and it becomes a substantial weight for just a handful of individuals to maneuver."

Ismail, nodding in agreement, acknowledged the formidable challenges posed by the Shroud's dimensions and weight. "Indeed, it's not something a lone thief could manage. This mastermind must have assembled a highly organized crew to pull off these daring thefts."

The conversation pivoted to the intricate planning and execution required for such a sophisticated operation. The involvement of a well-coordinated team equipped with the knowledge of the Shroud's dimensions and the security measures in place underscored the level of finesse behind the heist. The duo recognized that unraveling the mystery of the stolen Shroud required not only uncovering the identity of the master thief but also understanding the intricate network that supported these audacious endeavors.

As Jeannie and Ismail delved deeper into their analysis, they couldn't help but marvel at the level of expertise required to orchestrate such elaborate thefts. The coordination, insider information, and ability to safely handle a relic of such substantial size and weight hinted at a criminal enterprise operating at the highest echelons of sophistication. The question lingered: who was the mastermind behind this audacious plot, and what motivated them to target these sacred artifacts?

The investigation unfolded as a puzzle, with each piece revealing a new layer of complexity. Jeannie and Ismail were determined to decipher the intricacies of the heist, but the shadowy presence of the master thief loomed large, leaving them grappling with more questions than answers. The pursuit of the truth became a race against time, with the stolen Shroud representing both mystery and urgency.

"Well, Ace, any ideas on our next move?" Jeannie inquired, attempting to push aside the troubling thought of her imminent hospice stay.

"Either we backtrack to Vincent D'Amico's castle and give the door a good pounding, hoping someone will finally answer, or we play the waiting game to see if the Phantom drops more breadcrumbs for us," Ismail suggested.

"That waiting game doesn't sound too shabby, but before we decide, I've got a little detour in mind," Jeannie said with an enigmatic grin.

Ismail raised an eyebrow, intrigued by Jeannie's mischievous expression. "And why, may I ask, are we making a pit stop at an electronic store?"

Jeannie leaned in, her eyes gleaming with a touch of guilt. "Imagine this scenario: we find ourselves once again at D'Amico's castle, and, once again, the only response we get is silence. Now, there's only one way in and out that I saw. So, my plan is simple—we swing by an electronic store and pick up a discreet alarm. We attach it to the door, and if it opens, we get a subtle heads-up that someone's on the premises."

Ismail grinned in approval. "Well, well, boss. That's not a half-bad idea. Let's turn the tables on this

Vincent D'Amico and make sure he and his crew can't slip away unnoticed."

Following yet another journey to Spain, with the castle appearing vacant once more, Jeannie, under Ismail's protective cover, discreetly installed the nearly invisible alarm system before they withdrew.

They found a hotel in the center of town and decided to grab an early dinner. Jeannie was requested by Darcy to check her emails since they had dug up more material on Vincent D'Amico. "Look at this information Darcy and Burk just sent us." She passed her laptop to Ismail, who began to read.

'Vincent D'Amico, the epitome of opulence, reveled in his status as a playboy born into the lap of luxury, a man whose wealth echoed through the corridors of old money. His lavish lifestyle was only rivaled by his professed passion for art, a self-proclaimed aficionado who traversed the globe in search of the most exquisite masterpieces. With an air of entitlement, he basked in the privilege afforded by his family's legacy.'

'Yet a darker truth lay beneath the veneer of sophistication. D'Amico's name was whispered in the shadows, linked with allegations of heinous crimes—murders and thefts that hinted at a sinister underbelly to his glamorous existence. It was a reality that seemed impervious to the claws of justice, as D'Amico effortlessly eluded the consequences of his actions time and again.'

For Darcy and Burk, Jeannie's IT experts, unveiling the layers of D'Amico's nefarious dealings had become a relentless pursuit. Each revelation painted a picture of a man who thrived on manipulation and deceit. The duo stumbled upon a trove of incriminating photographs, capturing D'Amico in the company of Natalia, a woman with a mysterious Russian last name. Rumors suggested that the Russian secret police, the FSB, harbored a keen interest in Natalia and sought to interrogate her.

'To those who crossed paths with Vincent D'Amico, he was often described as a narcissist of unparalleled proportions. His insatiable appetite for power and possession knew no bounds, and he would stop at nothing to satiate his desires.' The enigma of D'Amico extended beyond the art world, weaving a complex tapestry of intrigue and danger that only intensified as Jeannie delved deeper into the web of secrets surrounding this charismatic yet menacing figure.

"So, what's the verdict?" Ismail inquired, handing the laptop back to Jeannie.

"I've got a gut feeling that taking down Vincent D'Amico and his entourage won't be a walk in the park," Jeannie replied with a discerning look.

Armed with a sniper scope, Delaney, stationed at the castle's front gate, had observed Jeannie and Ismail from a vantage point hundreds of yards away. He suspected that Jeannie had implemented a device to notify them when D'Amico and his associates returned. "Impressive move, Jeannie," Delaney mused to himself." A tad deceptive, but I can't help but admire it."

The tension in the air lingered as Delaney continued his surveillance, recognizing the strategic brilliance behind Jeannie's actions. As he observed the unfolding chess game, it became clear that facing D'Amico required not just cunning but a willingness to embrace a certain level of guile. Delaney couldn't help but appreciate the calculated risks being taken, understanding that deception often walked hand-in-hand with survival in the world they inhabited.

CHAPTER TWENTY-FOUR

The GPS guided D'Amico and his entourage precisely to the coordinates provided by Cardinal Mahoney. The late hour rendered the narrow street desolate, cloaked in darkness. D'Amico rapped softly on the door, and it swung open to reveal Mahoney. In the shadows, Natalia's readiness to draw her weapon was evident.

"Cardinal Mahoney," D'Amico greeted, stepping into the small cottage-like dwelling with Natalia in tow. "I assume you've brought my payment?" he inquired, eyes flickering to the two other Cardinals. "And who might these individuals be?" he pressed.

Mahoney introduced the newcomers. "This is Cardinal McCormick and Cardinal Vallini. Can we proceed with the inspection of the Shroud?"

"You may, but my question remains unanswered. Do you have my payment?" D'Amico insisted, a subtle edge to his tone.

"Yes, we have your payment, but we'll only release it after we've examined the relic," Cardinal McCormick asserted sternly.

"Very well, then. Follow me, gentlemen," D'Amico said, motioning for Natalia to exercise patience. His plan unfolded silently in his mind—to present the Cardinals with a glimpse of the Shroud and then, upon returning to the cottage, extract the agreed-upon payment before eliminating all three Cardinals. The clandestine dance of power and deception was set to continue in the dimly lit confines of that secluded cottage.

As Miguel observed their approach, he gracefully exited the driver's seat and swung the rear door of the van open, triggering the overhead lights to cast an illuminating glow. The trio of Cardinals stood before the shroud, its linen surface bearing the distinct facial impression presumed to be that of Jesus. In a synchronized gesture, the three men made the sign of the cross, each reverently kissing a corner of the sacred relic's container.

D'Amico, his tone laced with sarcasm, couldn't resist a dry comment, "So, are you three satisfied with the merchandise?" he quipped. "If that's the case, perhaps we can now make our way back to the cottage so I can collect my payment." His gaze flickered towards Natalia, silently signaling her to be prepared for what was to come.

The atmosphere hung heavy with anticipation as D'Amico navigated the delicate dance between mockery and business. The sacred artifact, bathed in the van's artificial light, served as an ethereal backdrop to the impending transaction. Little did the Cardinals suspect that beneath D'Amico's apparent compliance lurked a calculated plan, one that would unfold in the dimly lit space of the cottage, where shadows concealed not only secrets but the imminent threat of treachery.

Once inside the cottage, Cardinal Mahoney disappeared into an adjacent room, returning with a substantial suitcase in tow. As D'Amico began to signal Natalia to initiate the planned elimination of the three Cardinals, Cardinal McCormick interjected, halting the impending action.

"Mr. D'Amico, before we proceed, there is one final relic we would like you to retrieve for us," Cardinal McCormick announced, causing D'Amico to grasp Natalia's arm just as she poised to draw her weapon.

"Another relic? Pray, enlighten me. I'm familiar with the Sudarium and, of course, the Shroud of Turin. What else is there?" D'Amico inquired, feigning curiosity.

"Are you acquainted with the True Cross?" Cardinal Vallini posed the question, and the three Cardinals exchanged glances before Vallini continued. "According to Christian tradition, the True Cross is believed to be the actual cross upon which Jesus of Nazareth was crucified. Historical accounts and legends tell of Helena, the mother of Roman Emperor Constantine the Great, discovering the True Cross at the Holy Sepulchre in Jerusalem between the years 326 and 328."

D'Amico, intrigued by the prospect of such a further significant artifact, dismissed Natalia's mounting frustration with a gesture. "And the Catholic Church is convinced it's genuine? Never mind, continue with your story. It piques my interest," he urged while Natalia, visibly bored, leaned against a wall.

Cardinal Vallini delved into the historical narrative, recounting how, during her pilgrimage, Saint Helena unearthed three crosses believed to have been used in the crucifixion of Jesus and the two thieves, Dismas and Gestas. According to late 4th-century historians Gelasius of Caesarea and Tyrannius Rufinus, one cross bore the titulus inscribed with Jesus' name. Helena, initially uncertain of its authenticity, reportedly witnessed a miracle that confirmed it as the True Cross.

"What kind of miracle are we talking about here?" Natalia interjected suddenly, her frustration giving way to genuine curiosity.

Cardinal McCormick studied Natalia before continuing, "Upon gazing upon the sacred site where the Savior had endured his suffering, the empress was moved with reverence. Without hesitation, she issued a decree for the immediate destruction of the idolatrous temple that had been built there by the

Muslims and commanded the removal of the very earth upon which it had been erected. As the debris of the pagan shrine was cast aside, a remarkable discovery unfolded. Buried near the Lord's Sepulchre were three crosses, hidden from sight for ages.

A collective certainty emerged in the people's hearts that one of these crosses had borne the form of our Lord Jesus Christ, while the other two had served as instruments of execution for the thieves crucified alongside him. Yet, a veil of uncertainty shrouded the identity of each cross—especially which one had been privileged to cradle the Body of the Lord and receive the precious outpouring of His divine blood.

The venerable and sagacious Macarius, the esteemed leader of the city, undertook the task of unraveling this enigma. With solemnity and profound devotion, he orchestrated a method to discern the true Cross among the trio. A lady of high standing, who had long suffered from a debilitating ailment, became the vessel for this divine inquiry. Each cross was brought into contact with her, accompanied by fervent prayers.

In a moment of divine revelation, the mystery was unveiled. The cross that had cradled the suffering body of the Lord emanated a virtuous power. As it drew near the ailing lady, a miraculous transformation occurred; the cross expelled the affliction that had plagued her, bringing about instant and profound healing. The miraculous touch of the True Cross became evident, and in that sacred moment, the veil of uncertainty was lifted, affirming the sanctity of the relic that had borne the weight of humanity's salvation."

Natalia derisively dismissed the narrative, earning herself a disapproving glare from D'Amico. "So, this True Cross holds great significance for your newfound Catholic Church?" D'Amico inquired.

Cardinal Vallini responded, "The Roman Catholic Church, Eastern Orthodox Church, Oriental Orthodox Church, and the Church of the East all lay claim to relics purported to be the True Cross, using them as revered objects. Meanwhile, Protestant and other Christian denominations generally cast doubt on the authenticity of such relics, holding them in lower esteem. However, to address your query directly, yes. The True Cross we are in pursuit of is of paramount importance to our faith, akin to the significance of the other two artifacts you've successfully acquired for us."

D'Amico scrutinized the image while Natalia peered over his shoulder. "It appears slightly larger than the Sudarium. I assume I'll need to take the base as well, considering it seems securely attached."

"Yes. Attempting to separate them could result in irreparable damage to the relic. So, are you prepared to help us one last time and secure the True Cross for the Church?" Cardinal Mahoney inquired.

"Yes, we will secure the relic for the agreed-upon price. However, unlike the Sudarium and the Shroud of Turin, this will require additional planning due to the current situation in the region. Let's carefully remove the Shroud from the van. I assume you have a prepared room?" D'Amico asked.

The group was escorted into the room from where Cardinal Mahoney had retrieved the suitcase, confirming that it was ready to house the Shroud. D'Amico glanced at Natalia and had to suppress a smile upon seeing the fake Sudarium securely on display.

After several attempts, D'Amico's crew, assisted by the three Cardinals, successfully maneuvered the Shroud into the room. D'Amico, with a scoff, couldn't help but inquire, "Out of curiosity, where do you intend to take these two relics and, soon, the True Cross? I presume you don't plan on keeping them here for eternity."

Uncertain about how much information to disclose, Cardinal McCormick responded that once a new Vatican City was constructed, their intention was to display all three relics to the faithful. D'Amico simply shrugged. "I'll be in touch once we have the True Cross. Just ensure you have my payment ready."

CHAPTER TWENTY-FIVE

Upon returning to the van, D'Amico instructed Natalia to check beneath the foam rubber to ensure the genuine Shroud was safely secured. After receiving a thumbs-up, they departed from the small town and made their way back to Spain. Although it was a lengthy drive, knowing that payment was in hand made it a pleasant journey.

"Do you honestly buy into all this nonsense about the True Cross possessing magical healing powers?" Natalia questioned, laying her head on D'Amico's chest in the back of the van.

"My dear Natalia, would you not agree that I am a pragmatic man?" D'Amico responded, not expecting a direct answer. "Let's approach this with reason. The Cardinals would have us believe that centuries after Christ's crucifixion, Queen Helena, Constantine the Great's mother, miraculously discovered the very cross on which Jesus was hung. Not only that, but she also stumbled upon two additional crosses that purportedly supported the thieves. And, to add a touch of authenticity, they claim that the True Cross healed a sick person on contact. I place as much belief in that tale as I do in the notion that the three Cardinals possess the genuine Sudarium and Shroud of Turin." Laughter echoed in the van at D'Amico's words.

He continued, "Let's be practical here. Legends often carry a weight of exaggeration, and I suspect these relics are no different. The allure of miracles adds value to their endeavor, but we're dealing with a business of belief, not necessarily fact."

As the van continued its journey, the engine's low hum provided a backdrop to the unfolding situation. Tim pivoted toward D'Amico with a sense of urgency. "Vincent, I've got a match on the individuals that arrived the other day at the castle using facial recognition," he reported, extending his laptop towards D'Amico. On the screen, a split image displayed a man and a woman.

D'Amico accepted the laptop, focusing on the images. "Who are they?" he inquired, his eyes narrowing as he studied the faces.

Tim pointed at the figures on the screen. "FBI agents. The woman is Agent Jeannie Loomis, and the man is her partner, Agent Ismail Flores. Both are highly decorated agents with impressive track records. If you open the second file, you can delve into their case histories."

D'Amico quickly accessed the second file, revealing a dossier showcasing the accomplishments of Agents Loomis and Flores. The pages chronicled a series of solved cases, each more intricate and high-profile than the last. D'Amico couldn't help but acknowledge the talent of the two agents, realizing that the individuals now in pursuit of the relics were no ordinary adversaries.

"Interesting," D'Amico mused, his mind processing the newfound information. "This complicates things, but it also adds a layer of excitement to our endeavors. We'll need to tread carefully and reconsider our strategy. What else do we know about these agents?" he inquired, returning his attention to Tim. The van rumbled along the road, the atmosphere inside becoming charged with the awareness that the stakes had just been raised.

"Both have accumulated many years of service with the FBI. Agent Loomis holds the position of Assistant Agent in Charge at their San Francisco office and holds a Ph.D. in Social Psychology. She was once an instructor in their behavioral analysis unit in Washington, D.C.," Tim explained, his eyes flickering between D'Amico and the laptop.

"I agree. Underestimating them would be a mistake. They've proven themselves to be exceptionally skilled at their craft. But the question remains: why are U.S. agents involved in the investigation of the Sudarium theft in Spain and the Shroud here in Italy?" Tim added.

D'Amico, his gaze fixed on the split screen displaying the photos of Loomis and Flores, absorbed the information without an immediate response. After a thoughtful pause, he finally spoke, "I concur, Tim. If my instincts are correct, we should anticipate their return once we're back at the castle. Our priority is to ensure there's no traceable evidence they can link to us. It's likely they were brought in by either Interpol or the Vatican, though at this point, it's mere speculation. They're in the dark for now, and we need to keep it that way."

As the van continued its journey, the atmosphere inside became charged with the awareness that the heist had taken an unexpected turn, now involving seasoned FBI agents whose motives and affiliations were yet to be fully unraveled. The need for caution and strategic planning became paramount in the face of this new and formidable challenge.

Delaney tracked the discreetly placed signal on the counterfeit Shroud to a charming town in Italy. Baffled by their unconventional choice, he contemplated the location of the authentic relic. Instead of heading back to the castle after the theft was reported, they had chosen to head for this unassuming cottage, prompting him to question the motive behind such a decision. Speculating that they might be delivering the fake for payment, a prospect he detested the thought of, Delaney couldn't shake his unease surrounding the unfolding events.

Maintaining a discreet distance, he trailed the van, careful not to raise suspicion among its occupants. Delaney calculated that unless they opted for an uninterrupted drive without motel stops, it would take several days for them to reach the castle. Faced with a potential disadvantage if they chose to drive straight through, he might have to abandon his surveillance. Fortunately, they decided to halt for the night and checked into a motel. D'Amico shared a room with Natalia, while the others dispersed, occupying two adjoining rooms, while the Sudarium was locked safely in the van.

Under the cover of the night, Delaney adopted a technique previously employed by Jeannie and Ismail at the castle. He affixed a more potent tracking device to the underside of the van. This strategic move ensured that in case he lost sight of the vehicle or lagged too far behind, locating it would be straightforward. Feeling secure in his anonymity, he checked into the same motel and called headquarters.

"Delaney," his supervisor answered. "We concur with your assessment regarding Vincent D'Amico's illicit trade of selling counterfeit relics for cash while covertly retaining the genuine articles, ostensibly for his personal gain. The green light for a raid on his castle and the subsequent return of the relics to the Catholic Church, likely the Vatican, is pending your request. Proceed when you're ready."

"Sir, I successfully tracked D'Amico and his crew to a small cottage in Italy last night. They removed the fake Shroud and placed it inside the residence, and three Catholic Cardinals assisted in carrying the object," Delaney reported.

"Cardinals?" exclaimed Delaney's supervisor. "What in the world are Cardinals doing with fake Church relics?"

"Sir, I don't believe they're aware of the switch. It appears they genuinely think they're in possession of the authentic items. I propose following D'Amico's team back to the castle to ascertain their next move," Delaney suggested.

"It's your call, Delaney, but we need to secure the Sudarium and Shroud as soon as possible, preventing D'Amico from reselling them," the supervisor emphasized before ending the call, leaving Delaney to ponder the unfolding mystery as he drifted off to sleep.

CHAPTER TWENTY-SIX

Jeannie's alert system pinged at three-thirty in the afternoon, signaling the main door of the castle had been opened. She promptly informed Ismail in his room, and the two wasted no time in hailing a cab for their swift return to D'Amico's residence.

Ismail voiced his concern as they sped toward their destination, "Do you think we should involve the Spanish police?"

Jeannie contemplated the idea. "I don't believe so," she replied. "The element of surprise is our ally in this situation. D'Amico is a seasoned master of thievery, and I doubt we'll discover any incriminating evidence immediately upon entering that would warrant an arrest. No, this is an opportunity to rattle his cage, hoping he panics and makes a mistake."

D'Amico and his crew had recently relocated the Shroud of Turin to the room adjacent to the dungeon that housed the Sudarium. As the group gathered around, admiring the two relics, a sudden flashing red light signaled activity at the front gate.

Natalia voiced her concern, "Should we hide?"

D'Amico shook his head. "No. If we ignore them, they'll persist, and considering today's close call with the Shroud in plain sight, it's better to engage. Let's entertain them, and maybe they'll reveal whatever information they have," D'Amico instructed the group.

Rushing upstairs, they dispersed into different rooms throughout the castle, leaving Vincent and Natalia to handle the approaching visitors at the gate. "Yes, can we help you?" D'Amico inquired, with Natalia discreetly concealing her handgun under her loosely fitted blouse, her arm casually draped around Vincent's waist.

Jeannie lifted her FBI badge, displaying it prominently as she introduced herself and Ismail. "Well, well, the Federal Investigation Bureau gracing my humble castle. Please, do come in," Vincent D'Amico remarked with a sly smile. "I'm genuinely intrigued to know what has brought such distinguished guests to my door."

As they entered, Vincent played the part of the gracious host, guiding them through the castle's opulent corridors and ornate rooms. "I must say,

I'm both honored and curious about your visit," he continued, gesturing expansively. "What could possibly have drawn the attention of the esteemed FBI to this quiet corner of the world?"

Jeannie and Ismail maintained watchful eyes, subtly scanning their surroundings for any signs of the missing relics. However, Vincent skillfully led them through a maze of rooms and passages, maintaining an air of hospitality while deflecting their inquiries. "This castle has been in my family for generations," he remarked, feigning nonchalance. "I'm sure you'll find it quite fascinating, even if I'm not entirely sure why you're here."

The tension escalated as the cat-and-mouse game continued, with Vincent skillfully guiding the conversation away from the true purpose of their visit. The castle, vast and mysterious, revealed no hints of the Sudarium or the Shroud, leaving Jeannie and Ismail with growing frustration. Yet, D'Amico's composure remained unyielding, and the castle's secrets seemed to elude their determined pursuit.

D'Amico finished leading them through the intricately decorated corridors of his opulent castle mansion until they arrived at the entrance of his lavishly appointed office. The aroma of expensive cigars lingered in the air as Ismail's eyes widened at the sight of the massive aquarium dominating one side of the room, its magnified fish seemingly dancing behind the transparent walls. The flickering light from the tank cast an eerie glow, creating an atmosphere that was both captivating and foreboding.

With a casual wave, D'Amico gestured for them to sit in the plush chairs opposite his grand mahogany desk. As they settled, he leaned back in his executive chair, steepling his fingers and fixing them with a calculating gaze. Ismail couldn't help but notice the subtle nuances in D'Amico's unspoken body language that hinted at a man accustomed to playing intricate games.

Once again, Ismail broached the purpose of their unexpected visit. "Mr. D'Amico, we appreciate the hospitality, but we're curious about something more specific. Are you truly just an art aficionado, or is there more beneath the surface?"

Jeannie, more observant than she let on, focused not on his words but on D'Amico's subtle shifts in posture, the way his eyes flitted across the room, and the rhythm of his responses. She continued the conversation, her tone casual yet probing, "We've heard rumors, you know. Whispers of a different kind of art—masterpieces that exist in the shadows, changing hands in ways that avoid the spotlight. You wouldn't happen to know anything about that, would you, Mr. D'Amico?"

D'Amico's lips curled into a half-smile, his eyes gleaming with a mix of amusement and defiance. "Agent Loomis, Agent Flores, you flatter me with your imagination. My interests are confined to beauty that can be openly appreciated, not the clandestine world you seem to be hinting at."

Jeannie leaned forward, her gaze unwavering. "You see, Mr. D'Amico, we're not here just for a chat about art; we're also here to understand the full spectrum of your endeavors. The kind that might not be captured on the pages of those impressive leather-bound books."

As the conversation continued, the air in the room thickened with tension, each word and gesture becoming a move in the intricate dance between law enforcement and a man who reveled in the shadows of his own creation.

The atmosphere resembled a tense game of chess, each player carefully considering their next move. Jeannie, however, was playing her cards close to her chest. She had a strategic aversion to broaching the topic of the Sudarium or Shroud of Turin. It was a delicate subject, and she sensed that revealing too much might tip the balance unfavorably.

Maintaining an air of nonchalance, she decided it was better to keep D'Amico guessing. As they all rose from their seats, expressions of gratitude painted on their faces, Jeannie and Ismail exchanged glances that communicated volumes without a single word. D'Amico extended his hand for a farewell shake, but neither agent reciprocated. There was a deliberate lack of physical contact, which was a subtle message in itself.

"Thank you, Mr. D'Amico, for the enlightening tour," Jeannie said, her voice composed. Ismail nodded in agreement, both agents exuding a sense of professional courtesy. Natalia, a silent observer throughout the encounter, followed them like a shadow as they made their way back through the castle's ornate corridors.

They reached the grand entrance that had welcomed them earlier. Jeannie turned to D'Amico with a gracious smile, "It's been a pleasure, Mr. D'Amico. We'll be in touch if we have any further questions."

As they stepped through the gate, a subtle tension lingered in the air, like the aftermath of a brilliant move on a chessboard. Natalia brought up the rear, her eyes scanning the surroundings with a vigilance that hinted at a deep layer of awareness. The agents maintained a composed façade, concealing the wheels turning in their minds.

Once beyond the gates, Jeannie couldn't help but glance back at the imposing construction. The pretense of civility and veneer of polite conversation had masked an intricate dance of wit and concealment. As they walked away, the chess match continued, the pieces rearranging on the board with every step, leaving the outcome hanging in the balance.

From his vantage point on the hill, Delaney felt a sense of satisfaction. He was the eyes and ears, the silent guardian of the secrets that lurked within D'Amico's castle. The thought of that hidden room in the dungeon gnawed at him. It was a puzzle piece that seemed to be missing from the grand tapestry of the investigation.

The agents' departure marked the beginning of a new phase in the dance. Delaney, ever the strategist, anticipated that D'Amico, now rattled by their unexpected visit, would be forced to reassess his moves. The chessboard of intrigue had been disrupted, and D'Amico, like a master tactician caught off guard, would need to adapt swiftly.

A torrent of thoughts surged through Delaney's mind as he maintained his vigilant watch. "What's your play with the Sudarium and Shroud now? Keeping them in the same place is no longer an option. What if Jeannie and Ismail decide to alert Spanish law enforcement and return armed with a search warrant? Moving them is imperative, but where to?"

The weight of uncertainty hung in the air as Delaney grappled with the urgency of the situation. The relics, once hidden in the shadows, were now at the center of a dangerous game. Every possible scenario played out in his mind – a desperate relocation, a covert transfer under the cover of darkness, or the selection of a new, unsuspecting sanctuary.

The castle, a temporary refuge for the enigmatic artifacts, was a vulnerable fortress. Delaney wondered if D'Amico truly grasped the solemnity of the issue. The possibility of law enforcement knocking on his door, armed with legal authority, was a looming threat that demanded a swift and decisive response.

As Delaney scanned the surroundings with his sniper scope, he pondered the intricacies of D'Amico's dilemma. "The game has changed," he murmured, his voice barely audible in the quiet of the night. "What will your next move be, D'Amico, to safeguard your secrets now that the spotlight is inching closer?"

The castle below remained a hive of covert activity. Delaney, perched on the hill, awaited the next chapter in this clandestine saga. The Sudarium and Shroud, once dormant artifacts with histories cloaked in mystery, had become pawns in a high-stakes chess game where the prizes were not just the pieces on the board but the very essences of secrets and deception.

Back in the castle, D'Amico convened an urgent meeting with his trusted associates. The atmosphere was charged with tension as they discussed the implications of Jeannie and Ismail's unexpected visit. D'Amico, usually composed and confident, now wore a furrowed brow that betrayed a hint of anxiety.

"They know we stole the relics. Their next recourse is to either notify the Spanish police or surveil our next move. We can't afford to underestimate them," he declared, his voice carrying an edge of urgency. "They know more than we anticipated. We need to secure our assets."

Delaney, still perched on the hill, adjusted his sniper scope and followed the movements below. "The game is afoot," he murmured to himself. "Let's see how D'Amico dances when the pieces are in motion."

As night fell, the castle's lights dimmed, concealing the clandestine operations within. Delaney remained vigilant, a lone sentinel watching the unfolding drama, waiting to decipher the next move in this high-stakes game where relics held secrets and every move had consequences.

The atmosphere in the castle was tense as the crew swiftly executed their leader's orders. Tim and Miguel wasted no time, quickly securing two additional vans to add to their resources. As the crew worked together, each member played their part in the intricate ballet of securing and transporting the authentic relics.

D'Amico's strategy was clear — to outmaneuver those who sought to intercept him. With three vans now at their disposal, the crew aimed to confuse their pursuers by loading only one with the valuable relics. The decision to leave the others empty would force their adversaries to make a choice, increasing the odds of successfully evading capture.

Time was of the essence, and D'Amico emphasized the need for speed. The concern about potential reinforcements from the opposing side compounded the risks. Every whispered conversation and hurried footstep in the opulent halls contributed to the symphony of activity, creating an atmosphere charged with anticipation.

The crew's synchronization was that of a well-drilled team, showcasing their professionalism and efficiency in handling the situation. As they prepared to execute their plan, the castle became a stage for this carefully choreographed operation, where every move and decision mattered in the high-stakes game they were playing.

"Bravo, D'Amico," exclaimed Delaney from his perch on the hill. "Jeannie and Ismail will undoubtedly be observing the unfolding activity and find themselves at a strategic disadvantage with just a single vehicle at their disposal."

"You'll play a masterstroke. First, you will roll out a van, a tempting bait for them to pursue. Then, you'll watch closely as they decide which one to tail. Once their move is revealed, you'll send out the second van and then the third. The question lingering in the air is which van will be carrying the authentic relics. Ah, that's where my trackers come into play. Their every move will be tracked, and every decision will be observed. The answer will be in my hands before they even realize they've fallen into our carefully set trap."

D'Amico's tone conveyed a sense of assurance as if the chess pieces on the board were already dancing to his orchestrated tunes. The room, filled with anticipation, seemed to be holding its breath and waiting for the climax of this high-stakes game of cat and mouse. Each calculated step and each strategic decision added a layer of complexity to the unfolding plot, making it clear that this operation was more than a simple heist; it was also a battle of wits, with D'Amico holding the board and dictating the rhythm of the impending showdown.

CHAPTER TWENTY-SEVEN

After Vincent D'Amico dispersed his crew to prepare for their getaway, he withdrew into his office, securing the door behind him. Scattered across his desk lay a detailed map delineating the intricate streets and alleyways of Jerusalem. The documents before him delved into the history of the Church of the Holy Sepulchre and the complex tale of the True Cross.

According to ancient accounts, when the body of Jesus was taken down from the Cross, the Cross itself was concealed in a ditch or well and covered with stones and earth to prevent discovery by his followers. Nearly three centuries later, in 312 A.D., as Constantine engaged in a fierce battle with Maxentius for control of the Roman Empire, he, not yet a Christian, prayed for divine intervention. In response, a radiant cross appeared in the sky, bearing the inscription "BY THIS SIGN YOU WILL CONQUER."

With victory secured at the Milvian Bridge on October 28, 312, Constantine, now indebted to God, mandated the symbol of Christianity on Roman standards and soldier's shields. The True Cross, believed to be the very one on which Jesus was crucified, was later discovered by Constantine's mother, St. Helena, in Jerusalem on September 14, 326. Guided by an aged Jew possessing traditional knowledge of the crucifixion site, the excavation revealed three crosses, the superscription from the Savior's head, and the crucifixion nails. The True Cross was distinguished when it miraculously revived a dead youth upon contact.

Vincent chuckled in the solitude of his office, noting the discrepancy in stories about the True Cross's miraculous powers. Undeterred, he continued his exploration of historical events.

In 614, King Chosroes II of Persia invaded Syria and Palestine, seizing numerous treasures, including the relic of the True Cross. Fifteen years later, in 629, Emperor Heraclius of Constantinople successfully recaptured the True Cross from Persia. In a display of penance, Heraclius personally carried the sacred cross back to Jerusalem clad in sackcloth and with bare feet. On September 14, the True Cross was reinstated in the Church of the Holy Sepulchre.

Natalia quietly entered Tim's room in a separate wing of the castle, her senses heightened by the sound of running water emerging from the bathroom. As she undressed, the anticipation in the air seemed to thicken. With each step, she got nearer to the bathroom, where steam wafted out from the partially open door. Amid this clandestine encounter, she glimpsed the enticing silhouette of Tim's body moving sensually beneath the shower head.

Upon opening the shower door and slipping inside, Natalia startled Tim, who was momentarily taken aback. Swiftly, she seized a washcloth, lathering it with soap, and began to tenderly wash Tim's chest. The warmth of the steam combined with the intimacy of the moment heightened the simmering tension between them, his excitement obvious under her touch.

In a hushed tone, Tim, his gaze fixed on the cascading water and Natalia's alluring figure, inquired, "Where's Vincent?"

"He's locked away in his office, immersed in his grand plans for our next heist," Natalia replied with a sly smile. "The man fancies himself a master planner of theft, but you and I know the truth. Without my ability to charm those with insider information, we wouldn't have laid our hands on either the Sudarium or the Shroud of Turin."

The clandestine conversation, punctuated by stolen touches and whispered plans, added an extra layer of tension to their plotting, blending desire with the dangerous game they were playing.

"So, what's our next move? I thought once we got the money from those three Cardinals, we'd be rid of Vincent and them and could settle up with the crew and make our way to South America," Tim whispered, his hands exploring Natalia's curves.

"Relax, I've got it all mapped out," Natalia reassured him. As they shared a moment of intimacy, she continued, "Once we've transitioned to our new hideout with the Sudarium and Shroud in tow, we'll let Vincent orchestrate our move to Jerusalem. Just like before, he'll rely on me to gather crucial inside information, and I'll play along. But this time, after we snatch the relic and have it safely stashed in our van, I'll take care of Vincent once and for all."

"But what about the rest of the crew? They'll be expecting their cut for those three successful thefts," Tim voiced his concern, the weight of the crew's expectations lingering in the air.

With a calculating gleam in her eye, Natalia responded, "Once the True Cross is safely stowed in the van, we'll make our way back to our concealed hideout. Once the relic is placed alongside the Sudarium and Shroud, I'll propose a toast. And after that, it'll be just the two of us."

Her sinister grin hinted at a dark and treacherous plan. As she spoke, Natalia skillfully played her seductive cards, her fingers teasingly working their way over Tim's body, bringing him to the edge of ecstasy. The room became a hidden setting for both the exchange of dangerous plots and the unspoken desires that fueled their illicit partnership.

Jeannie's cell phone vibrated on the bar table at which she and Ismail were seated. Glancing at the Caller ID, she noted it was Lomax. She looked at Ismail before answering, saying, "It's the boss."

"Jeannie, I just received another anonymous email similar in nature to the ones we got during the Hitler clone investigation," Lomax explained.

"Hold on a minute. Let me put you on speakerphone so Ismail can hear. Okay, go ahead," Jeannie responded.

"Alright, here it is. It's addressed to me, SAC Lomax. By now, your agents have likely discovered that the mastermind behind the thefts of the Sudarium and the Shroud of Turin is a Vincent D'Amico and his crew. He has a castle in Spain, where the two relics are currently stored. However, he has a different motivation. He's been using artificial intelligence to replicate the relics, which he then sells to three Cardinals from the Catholic Church for huge sums, while keeping the originals for himself."

Jeannie exchanged a glance with Ismail, realizing that Lomax was conveying information that started to fill in pieces of the puzzle they were grappling with. Lomax continued.

"These three Cardinals are from the Vatican, and from what I've learned from various sources, they are attempting to use the relics for the formation of a new Catholic Church made up of traditional Catholics unhappy with the liberal direction in which Pope Francis is taking the institution. Soon, D'Amico and his team will leave the castle for an unknown new location. They'll attempt to play a shell game, sending out three identical vans in different directions to confuse the limited police resources in the area. Tell your agents not to fret, as I've placed a tracking device on one of the relics and will notify you as soon as I find their new location. That's the end of the email," Lomax said.

"Who is this guy? A spy? And how did he gain access to the castle?" Ismail inquired.

"All good questions," Jeannie replied. "I think we need to start heading back toward D'Amico's lair. I'll fill you in later, boss," Jeannie began to say, but Lomax interrupted, urging the two of them to stay safe.

CHAPTER TWENTY-EIGHT

"Alright, let's move out!" Vincent's commanding voice echoed through the air, rallying everyone present. Natalia gracefully climbed into the van alongside Vincent, with Miguel once again at the wheel. Tim took the driver's seat in the second van, which housed the remaining crew members. The third van, skillfully maneuvered by Marco, safeguarded the two precious relics.

From the vantage point of the hillside, Delaney observed the synchronized departure of the three vans as they navigated down a narrow one-lane road, eventually arriving at a pivotal three-way intersection. "Okay, assholes, this is where you'll split up," Delaney mumbled to the soft breeze, his gaze fixed on the unfolding scene.

Jeannie and Ismail sat in a cab down at the intersection, partially concealed by a florist shop. They had instructed the driver to follow the second van, their decision guided by the information gleaned from Lomax's email. Their anticipation heightened as they prepared to tail one of the vans, uncertain if it was the correct one.

As the vans approached the crossroads, Miguel steered his van straight ahead while the second van took a right turn and the third van veered left. D'Amico, glancing in a side mirror, caught sight of a cab swiftly tailing the second van. A wry smile played on his lips as he remarked, "Good morning, FBI," and then punctuated his words with laughter that resonated within the confines of the van. The game of cat and mouse had officially begun, with the winding roads and hidden agendas propelling them into a high-stakes pursuit.

Several miles along the road, Marco skillfully closed the gap behind the first van, and they reached their designated safe house after forty-five minutes of driving. Upon arrival, they swiftly extracted the Sudarium. However, they had to patiently wait for Tim and the rest of the crew to arrive before tackling the more cumbersome task of transporting the much heavier Shroud into the hideout's secure confines.

Tim guided the second van to a small roadside café where, under Jeannie and Ismail's vigilant gazes, he unlocked the rear door, allowing several men to exit. "Obviously, we picked the wrong van," Ismail remarked. "I was never good at playing that shell game. Now what?" he queried Jeannie.

"Well, we head back to our hotel and wait until we get new information. What bothers me the most about this cat-and-mouse routine is that, so far, we've never had any leverage. We're always in a position of waiting, whether for D'Amico's move or another cryptic email to guide us," Jeannie expressed, frustration evident in her voice as the onset of another headache loomed.

Tim dialed D'Amico's number, providing him with an update on the cab surveillance that had recently given up and departed the area. Additionally, he offered an estimated time of arrival at their new location.

D'Amico's new choice of hideout gave Delaney ample options for operating covertly while watching their every move. "Must be waiting for more manpower to move the Shroud into the residence," he thought. A short time later, his speculation was validated with the arrival of the third van. Immediately, Vincent ordered them to bring in the Shroud of Turin.

The entire crew reconvened in the largest of the three rooms within the house, where D'Amico and Natalia awaited their return. D'Amico addressed the group, his voice carrying an air of authority, "Gentlemen, I apologize for the limited space in this temporary accommodation compared to my beloved castle. We will only be here for tonight.

"Tomorrow, we embark on a journey to the State of Israel, our destination being Jerusalem. This marks our last heist, and rest assured, it will be our most challenging. Yet, the reward awaiting us will set us all up for life." The room erupted in cheers, the prospect of the impending venture resonating among the crew members. The anticipation and energy within the room mirrored the enormity of the heist they were about to undertake—one that promised both great risk and unparalleled rewards.

D'Amico signaled for Natalia to join him in an adjoining room and instructed Tim to fetch pizza and drinks for the entire crew. As they entered the room, D'Amico cast a searching gaze at Natalia, an intensity that stirred a sense of unease within her. The apprehension hung in the air, making her wonder if he had somehow unraveled the intricate dynamics between her and Tim.

"I'm afraid this time, you'll need to leverage all your seductive prowess," D'Amico declared, his words causing a surge of panic in Natalia. She began to second-guess herself, fearing that D'Amico had indeed connected the dots about her and Tim.

Easing the tension, D'Amico continued, "I have no specific suggestions on how you can obtain the insider information we need. The Holy Sepulchre is in the shittiest part of the world."

Natalia, now relieved that D'Amico hadn't confronted her about her relationship with Tim, listened intently. The room became a clandestine space where plans were discussed and uncertainties loomed. The upcoming heist, set against the backdrop of Jerusalem's profound historical significance, demanded a unique set of skills and strategies. The air was charged with the weight of expectations, and Natalia knew that her captivating charm would play a pivotal role in the success of their daring endeavor.

Vincent approached Natalia with deliberate intent, his hands skillfully unbuttoning her silk blouse. Natalia, well-versed in the art of deception, engaged in the charade of being a willing participant, allowing Vincent's touch to play across her skin. Deep within, she harbored the knowledge that this performance marked the culmination of a deceptive game—a game she had played with calculated precision, knowing this would be the final time she would have to appease him.

As the silk fell away, revealing a canvas of vulnerability, Natalia maintained her façade, concealing her true intentions. Her mind, however, raced with her anticipation of the impending conclusion when the tables would turn, and she could free herself from the constraints of this manipulative dance. The room, bathed in a deceptive intimacy, became a stage for the culmination of a plan that had been meticulously orchestrated, with the final notes of a symphony playing in the background.

Their journey to Jerusalem stretched across vast distances, yet the necessary paperwork for entering Israel smoothly passed inspection. The group, now on foreign soil, secured accommodations at a hotel conveniently situated near the Church of the Holy Sepulchre. As the team settled in, D'Amico once again gathered them that afternoon to deliver his final directives before embarking on their ultimate heist.

"I've recently gleaned valuable information through Natalia's impressive seductive talents. There lies another artifact beyond the primary relic we're set to steal: a significant portion of the sign that adorned the Cross bearing the inscription 'Jesus of Nazareth, King of the Jews.' While our benefactor hasn't explicitly tasked us with securing this object, we shall do so nonetheless."

He directed Tim to set up a screen and activate a laptop before continuing with his talk. "This won't be as smooth or tidy as the thefts of the Sudarium and the Shroud. The presentation I'm about to show you outlines what we'll be dealing with in a few hours," he announced, signaling for Tim to advance to the next slide.

"According to traditions dating back to the 4th century, this site holds two locations revered in Christianity. One is the place where Jesus was crucified, known as Calvary or Golgotha, and two is Jesus' empty tomb, the site of his burial and resurrection. With each reconstruction of the church, antiquities from the prior structure were incorporated into the newer renovation. Now, onto the next point," he instructed.

"Don't worry. I understand this information can be overwhelming," he reassured the team, acknowledging the complexity of the task ahead.

Plan of the Basilica of the Holy Sepulchre

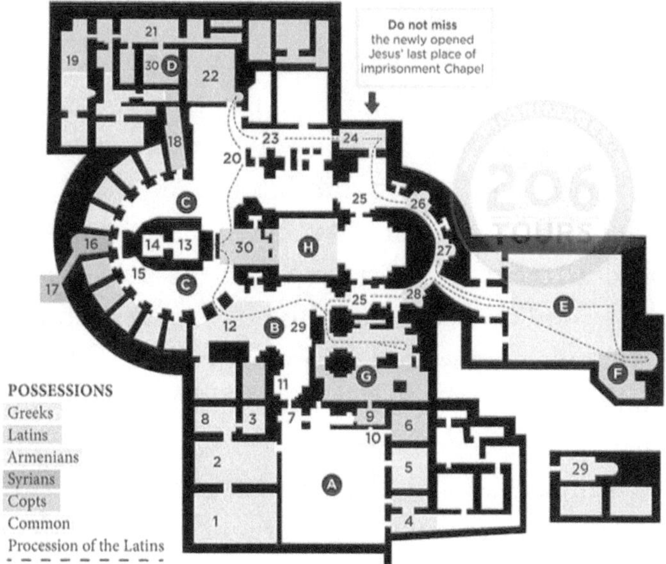

1. Chapel of St. James
2. Chapel of St. John the Ev.
3. Chapel of 40 Martyre
4. Convent of St. Abraham
5. Chapel of St. John the B.
6. Chapel of St. Michael
7. Belfry
8. Chapel of the Franks
10. Chapel of St. Mary of Egypt
11. Moslem Divan
12. Place of the Holy Women
13. Chapel of the Angel
14. The Sepulchre
15. Chapel of the Copts
16. Chapel of the Syrians
17. Jewish Tomb
18. Passage
19. Cistern
20. St. Mary Magdalen
21. Franciscan Convent
22. Latin Sacristy
23. Arches of the Virgin
24. Prison of Christ
25. Corridor
26. St. Longinus
27. Division of the Mocking
28. Cave of Adam
29. Plan of the Chapel of Adam
30. Franciscan Choir

A. Atrium
B. Stone of Anointing
C. Holy Sepulchre
D. Chapel of the Apparition
E. Chapel of St. Helen
F. Chapel of Holy Cross
G. Calvary
H. Greek Choir

"I captured this image yesterday during a tour Natalia and I took of the site," he began, employing a laser pointer to guide his crew through the floorplan. "This is Calvary, or 'Golgotha,' the precise location where the Cross supposedly stood and where Jesus Christ sacrificed himself for our sins. Pilgrims can kneel at this altar inside the Church of the Holy Sepulchre, reaching out to touch the exact spot where Our Savior's earthly journey concluded before his miraculous Resurrection.

"Now, let's delve into the Edicule, the Tomb of Christ within the Church of the Holy Sepulchre, as you can see here. There are two chambers within this space. The first is the 'Chapel of the Angel,' showcasing a stone that was part of the large stone rolled away from Christ's tomb on Easter morning. The second chamber is the 'Tomb of Christ,' housing the marble slab where Jesus' body was laid. A vase of candles marks the place where his head rested and a banner suspended over the slab changes based on the liturgical seasons. This stands as the most Holy Catholic site globally, the very place where Jesus supposedly rose from the dead."

"Now, here is our prize," D'Amico said as he motioned Tim to proceed. The slide showed the relic.

"At first glance, it might not look like much, but our benefactors are compensating us generously for its possession. It should be a straightforward extraction; it's not attached to a substantial base, so I don't foresee any issues," Vincent explained to his team. "Natalia has managed to secure the security codes that Tim will use to circumvent their security systems. Alright, we leave at 1 a.m., so try and get some rest."

Jeannie and Ismail touched down in Israel after a hectically arranged flight, spurred on by Lomax's recent email instructing them to head there. Eager to familiarize themselves with the surroundings and gain insight into their mission, they embarked on a tour of the Holy Sepulchre. The visit not only provided them with a better understanding of the terrain but also afforded them a glimpse of the revered True Cross.

Surveying the sacred surroundings, Ismail couldn't help but express his astonishment in a hushed tone to Jeannie, "So, how many damn relics does this guy want?" The weight of their mission in this holy place hung in the air, and Ismail's whispered question reflected the enormity of the task at hand.

"I forgot about the True Cross, mainly because there seem to be so many 'authentic' pieces circulating among various individuals and churches," Jeannie admitted, her voice reflecting a mix of skepticism and contemplation. "Unlike the Sudarium and the Shroud, where there is a consensus supporting their authenticity, the True Cross is shrouded in ambiguity. The story of St. Helena and her discovery of the three crosses adds an element of uncertainty. It's a challenge to discern the true relic among the myriad claims," she continued, recognizing the complexity of their mission in the face of conflicting narratives surrounding the True Cross.

"I don't follow," Ismail said.

"When it comes to holy relics, no one seems to hold back on claims. We've got supposed nails from the crucifixion, pieces of the throne of crowns, and the list goes on," Jeannie remarked, her tone tinged with a blend of irony and contemplation. "The authenticity of these relics is often questionable, and it becomes a murky territory to navigate. Except for the Sudarium and the Shroud, where we've found a more solid ground of consensus, the world of holy relics is filled with ambiguity. It's as if everyone wants a piece of the divine, and who's to say what's genuine and what's not?" Jeannie shared her musings with Ismail, acknowledging the complexities of their mission in the realm of sacred artifacts.

CHAPTER TWENTY-NINE

Unbeknownst to Jeannie and Ismail, in the clandestine hush of the night, Delaney skillfully positioned himself outside the revered Church of the Holy Sepulchre as the clock struck 1 a.m. A mysterious air enveloped the scene, heightened by the haunting echoes of a Muslim prayer that reverberated through the stillness, adding an unforeseen layer of complexity to the unfolding drama.

As Delaney observed the duo assuming their positions diagonally across from him, the ethereal melody of the prayer seemed to intertwine with his contemplative thoughts. "Well, Jeannie," he murmured inwardly, his voice a mere whisper against the backdrop of the echoing prayer, "how do you and Ismail intend to navigate this intricate situation?"

The ambient sounds of the night, including the rhythmic cadence of the prayer, underscored the moment. Delaney pondered the unfolding events, his mind navigating the delicate balance required to ensure a successful resolution. "Perhaps," he ruminated, "it would be prudent to allow D'Amico and his associates to proceed with their planned theft. Shadowing them discreetly back to their clandestine lair might unveil a trove of invaluable information."

Delaney, aware of the potential consequences, recognized that confronting the perpetrators directly at the Church could escalate into a perilous confrontation – an undesirable scenario for all parties involved.

The haunting melody continued to weave through the silent night, a juxtaposition to the strategic musings within Delaney's mind. As he maintained his covert vigil, the Church of the Holy Sepulchre stood as a silent witness to the unfolding drama, bathed in the pale moonlight, while the hidden chess match played out beneath the veiled canopy of the early morning hour.

The night air hung heavy with anticipation as the trio clandestinely observed the approach of two identical vans, their engines humming softly in the stillness. Silhouetted against the dimly lit backdrop of the Church of the Holy Sepulchre, the vans rolled in slowly, their presence shrouded in an air of mystery. The tension in the air escalated as the onlookers waited in the shadows, eyes fixed on the unfolding scene.

As the vans came to a halt, a lone figure emerged from the lead vehicle, a penlight clenched between his teeth. The observers' pulses quickened as the figure, a male of calculated demeanor, approached the church with purpose. With deft precision, he punched in a code on a concealed panel, a subtle dance of shadows and light playing out in the secret exchange. The coded entry opened a gateway, granting access to the church's inner sanctum.

Turning back to the vans, the mysterious figure signaled an all-clear for the crew to proceed. Miguel and Marco, guardians of the vehicles, stood vigilant as D'Amico, Natalia, and the rest of the crew stealthily made their way into the hallowed halls of the first building.

Inside, a hushed tension prickled around them as the crew conducted a swift search, finding the building devoid of any unwanted visitors. The subdued glow of candlelight, remnants of a day's devotion, provided just enough illumination to navigate the space without the need for intrusive flashlights. The thieves moved with calculated precision, their every step echoing with the gravity of the impending crime.

D'Amico, sensing the proximity of their coveted prize, raised a hand in silent command, halting the advance of his accomplices. As the crew gathered around, he cast an ominous gaze upon the relic they sought – the True Cross. A collective hush fell over the group.

Breaking the silence, D'Amico motioned for Tim, a tech-savvy member of the crew, to act. Tim, upon laying eyes on the revered relic, approached an adjacent wall where a concealed panel awaited. With practiced skill, he bypassed a few circuits, a silent acknowledgment passing between him and D'Amico. The nod signaled that the security system had been successfully disarmed, a crucial step in the unfolding heist that would determine the success or failure of their daring mission. The stage was set, and the stolen whispers of the night hinted at the impending climax of a clandestine operation fraught with suspense.

Someone's voice reverberated from the shadowy corner of the room in Arabic, a cryptic utterance that marked the final words from an unsuspecting figure. In the blink of an eye, Natalia swiftly silenced him with a single shot, the suppressed weapon ensuring lethal precision as the man crumpled to the floor, his life extinguished in an instant. The room, now tainted with the scent of gunpowder, continued to function with a militaristic discipline, with each member of the crew absorbed in their assigned tasks.

As the crew orchestrated their retreat after securing the prized True Cross, D'Amico delved into the historical and religious significance of the stolen artifact. He raised the titulus, revealing the faint but still discernible letters 'INRI,' translating to "Jesus the Nazarene, King of the Jews" in English. When he was mid-this revelation, D'Amico looked up to find Natalia with her gun leveled at him in a sudden twist in the plot that defied his expectations.

Perplexed, D'Amico questioned her, but his initial assumption that this was some macabre game was quickly dispelled. "What are you doing?" he inquired, a note of immediacy in his voice. "We must hurry back to the van and escape."

A chilling calm settled over Natalia as she seized the moment to reveal long-buried grievances. "Vincent, I have long grown weary of being nothing more than your sexual pawn, catering to your whims at a moment's notice," she declared, her voice cutting through the charged atmosphere. "However, even more intolerable is your callous exploitation of me as a means to gather insider information for every theft we've executed – whoring me out to anyone as long as I succeeded.

"The moment has arrived for the true mastermind to take command of both the revered relics and the proceeds we've garnered. Farewell." A resounding shot pierced the air, finding its mark in D'Amico's forehead, extinguishing his life in an instant. He crumpled to the floor, the same ground that had previously borne the weight of the sacred True Cross.

Natalia picked up the titulus and secured it under her shirt. She meticulously retraced her steps, weaving through the shadows back to where the vans awaited their hasty escape. The air was thick with tension as she approached, the crew members casting questioning glances as they awaited the return of their leader. Inquisitively, one of the crew members asked, "Where's Vincent?"

Natalia met the query with a cool demeanor, her response swift and measured. "Didn't you hear the gunshot?" she replied, a hint of urgency in her voice. "There was an armed guard on the scene. He took a shot at Vincent, and I retaliated, neutralizing the threat. But when I rushed to Vincent's side, he was dead."

Unease settled among the crew, their expressions reflecting a mixture of concern and disbelief. The unexpected turn of events had injected an element of uncertainty into their meticulously planned operation. As Natalia continued to recount the perilous encounter, the night air seemed to carry an undercurrent of suspense, leaving the crew to grapple with the abrupt absence of their erstwhile leader. The clandestine mission once shrouded in the certainty of meticulous planning, now unfolded with an unforeseen twist that hinted at the unpredictable nature of their criminal escapade.

"Hurry. We must quickly get out of here. Someone must have surely heard the shots. Let's get back to our hideout and secure the two relics." She pulled out the titulus and handed it to one of the other members. "Put this with the True Cross. I'm sure we will get a handsome price for it."

As the two vans cautiously left the area, Jeannie and Ismail looked on, as did Delaney. "Nice move, Jeannie. I will let you know where you can find the relics soon," he thought as he retreated from the rooftop.

CHAPTER THIRTY

This time, in a departure from their usual protocol, the vans moved in unison toward their newly designated hideout in a convergence of darkness and secrecy. Natalia, sensing the need for heightened caution, directed the crew urgently upon their arrival.

"Quickly, we must secure the Sudarium and the Shroud of Turin in the van alongside the True Cross and titulus," Natalia instructed, her voice laced with a practical edge. "One van traveling along a night road attracts far less attention than a pair, especially after what just transpired."

The crew, responding to her directive with practiced efficiency, extracted the revered relics from their protective concealment. The Shroud of Turin and the Sudarium were carefully placed in the van, joining the True Cross and its accompanying titulus. A sense of accomplishment mingled with an air of solemnity, knowing that the success of their heist hinged on the precision of their movements in the cloak of the night.

With the relics secured, Natalia, the de facto leader in Vincent's absence, proposed a symbolic gesture to honor their fallen comrade. "Once we're back at the hideout, I will host a toast to our remarkable achievement tonight and pay our respects to Vincent," she announced, her words carrying a gravity that resonated in the dimly lit space.

As they returned to the hideout, Natalia took charge once more, this time pouring wine into several cups. The atmosphere was tense yet celebratory, a paradoxical blend of success and the looming shadows of their actions. "To Vincent and a lifetime of wealth," she toasted, raising her cup. The crew followed suit, participating in the bittersweet ritual of acknowledgment and revelry.

In a calculated move, as soon as Natalia and Tim finished their drinks, they smashed their cups against the table. A symbolic act, they hoped others would follow suit, and indeed, the crew emulated their actions. The mood shifted, and shortly, several members began to choke and stumble, suffering the effects of a carefully administered substance.

In the orchestrated chaos that ensued, Natalia and Tim moved strategically, adapting to their drugged companions' unpredictable movements. As the crew succumbed to the poison, one by one, they lay on the floor, with Natalia and Tim looking on with a mix of satisfaction and justification, knowing this was the final act in a night rife with intrigue and peril.

"So, do we make our getaway now?" Tom inquired, his gaze shifting to the bodies sprawled on the floor. Natalia shook her head. "No, not yet. We need to unwind and get a decent night's sleep." With a deliberate nonchalance, she started unbuttoning her blouse, removing it with a subtle grace. "You and I need to celebrate," she added, striding over to Tom and skillfully unbuckled his pants, sensing the heightened anticipation in the air.

Delaney methodically traversed the adjacent residences until he arrived at the van. Confirming it was securely locked, he mused, "So much for safeguarding the artifacts in a controlled setting." Turning his attention to the front door of the house, he noted sufficient illumination from the streetlights and the moon, rendering a flashlight unnecessary. Every nerve in his body was alert; he was acutely aware that D'Amico's body hadn't been discovered in the church yet. Presuming the man had met his fate there, given his absence during the crew's exit, Delaney now pondered the whereabouts of the remaining members within their escape refuge.

Turning the doorknob cautiously, Delaney was taken aback to find the door swinging open without resistance. A hush enveloped the surroundings, which were devoid of any discernible voices, as he paused, attuning to the stillness for a few minutes. The interior lay cloaked in darkness, which was in stark contrast to the moonlit night outside, prompting him to reach for his compact flashlight. Gripping his automatic firmly in his right hand, he gingerly pushed the door ajar.

The feeble beam of light revealed a grim scene within the main room — several lifeless bodies were strewn across the floor, each in a different, sickening pose. The shadows seemed to dance eerily around the motionless figures, casting an unsettling atmosphere over the sinister space.

Navigating around the lifeless forms that occupied the main room, Delaney approached a closed door leading to an adjoining room. Curiosity piqued, he gently pressed his ear against the door, and to his surprise, the muffled sounds of intimate passion reached him. A distinct male and female presence hinted at their engagement in amorous activities. Fueled by a mix of incredulity and curiosity, he cautiously eased the door open, revealing a scene of carnal connection within.

The room's ambiance resonated with the rhythmic cadence of the couple's ardor. The unmistakable sounds suggested that the female participant occupied the dominant position, orchestrating a passionate dance atop the male counterpart. Two candles, their flickering flames casting dancing shadows, provided a dim but revealing glow, aiding Delaney's vision in this unexpected voyeuristic moment. The subdued lighting added an unexpected layer of complexity to the secret setting as the door creaked open. Delaney found himself inadvertently peering into a private moment that was in stark contrast to the grim discovery he had made moments earlier.

Delaney patiently bided his time in the dark shadows, deciding to wait until the fervent pair reached the pinnacle of their passion. His rationale was to ensure that any potential threat posed by their heightened energy would be spent, providing him with a tactical advantage. The crescendo of their intimacy reached its zenith, marked by the more vociferous female participant announcing her satisfaction and rolling off the now-spent male.

Seizing the opportune moment, Delaney moved swiftly. With a deft push, he swung the door open, temporarily blinding the disoriented couple with the piercing beam of his flashlight. As they fumbled to recover, he located a nearby light switch, bathing the room in illumination.

However, the abrupt intrusion triggered a swift response from the male, who revealed a concealed firearm from under his pillow. In one decisive motion, Delaney fired a single shot, eliminating the immediate threat. Natalia, horrified, let out a scream as she witnessed the bedsheet and pillow rapidly staining with crimson. Desperation drove her to reach for a weapon on a nearby nightstand, but a stern warning from Sean halted her in her tracks.

Ignoring her lack of modesty, Natalia moved away from Tim's lifeless form, casting a disdainful sneer at Delaney. "Who the hell are you? Do you get your kicks by watching people fuck?" she spat, her voice laced with a mixture of shock and defiance.

Delaney stepped into the room, purposefully closing the door behind him to create an air of confidentiality. "Would you like to get dressed?" he inquired calmly.

Natalia's response was swift and laced with defiance. "Fuck you. What do you want?" she retorted, her tone a mixture of aggression and apprehension. Without hesitation, she swung her legs off the bed, starkly nude, and began advancing toward the nightstand with her back turned to Delaney.

His response was measured but firm, "I told you. Reach for your gun, and you'll join your lover here." The threat hung heavily in the air, freezing Natalia in her tracks. In a sudden moment of vulnerability, she retreated to the bed, now clutching the sheet to hastily cover herself. The tension in the room seemed to contract.

"So, what do you want?" Natalia demanded, her eyes narrowing in suspicion, a mix of fear and curiosity etched across her face. The dim light accentuated the shadows playing on the room's contours, creating an atmosphere charged with uncertainty and a foreboding sense of consequence.

Delaney maintained his composure in the face of Natalia's defiance. "I would like you to provide me with some answers. Where is Vincent D'Amico?" he inquired, his gaze unwavering.

Natalia responded with a calculated tone of sarcasm, "Who is Vincent D'Amico?" Her feigned innocence was palpable, a mask veiling any acknowledgment of the name. "You've broken into the wrong house. Leave now before I call the police," she declared, attempting to assert authority and dismiss the gravity of the situation.

Undeterred, Delaney continued, "Vincent D'Amico. A man involved in matters that transcend the ordinary. I know he's connected to this operation. Where is he?" His words carried a weight of urgency and determination as if the revelation of D'Amico's whereabouts held the key to unraveling a complex puzzle. The room, bathed in a surreal mix of artificial and moon-borne light, seemed to tense up again, the air thick with an unspoken potential for confrontation.

Delaney, resolute and unyielding, closed the distance between himself and Natalia. Without a word, he pressed the cold metal of the suppressor against her right knee. The room fell into a chilling silence, broken only by the weight of his ultimatum.

"I will ask one more time," Delaney declared, his voice low and unwavering. "If you do not tell me what happened to your leader, I will shoot you in the knee. You will never walk normally again." The gravity of his words hung in the air, each syllable laden with the potential for irreversible consequence.

Natalia felt the stark reality of the situation pressing against her. The cold touch of the suppressor against her knee was a tangible reminder of the power Delaney held at that moment. Her eyes darted between his face and the gun, grappling with the severity of the choice before her. The room, bathed in a muted glow, witnessed the tension escalating to a breaking point as the fate of her mobility rested in her decision.

A chilling laugh escaped Natalia's lips, a sound that echoed with a disturbing mix of mockery and disdain. "My leader. He was not my leader," she scoffed, her tone dripping with contempt. "He was an egotistical asshole who reveled in collecting things of value, using pawns like me to obtain them. But he's no longer among the living."

Her eyes, cold and unyielding, betrayed no hint of remorse. As if relishing the revelation, she continued with ruthless precision, "Vincent D'Amico met his end in a place of supposed sanctuary, a church. How fitting for a man who sought redemption through his sins." The words rolled off her tongue with detached cruelty as if the demise of the once-powerful figure brought her a satisfaction that transcended the boundaries of humanity. The room seemed to absorb the venom in her voice, heightening the atmosphere of malevolence that lingered between her and Delaney.

CHAPTER THIRTY-ONE

Jeannie, absorbed in her struggles with an unrelenting headache, initially failed to perceive the faint vibrations of her cell phone on the nightstand, the rhythmic pulsing drowned out by her oppressive discomfort. Stumbling into the bathroom, she found herself grappling with waves of nausea, the pills proving ineffective against the relentless assault of pain.

In a moment of desperation, she vocalized her plea, "Please, God, help me solve this case and return home. This is all I ask. I am in your hands." The words uttered aloud in the quiet solitude of the bathroom carried a weight of sincerity and vulnerability.

Rinsing her mouth with mouthwash, a seemingly routine act became an inadvertent trigger for her queasiness, compounding her physical distress.

Nevertheless, she gathered herself and returned to the nightstand, discovering a text message from Lomax that bore an address. A surge of urgency propelled her to dial Ismail's room, instructing him to prepare and meet her in the lobby immediately. "A lead has just been emailed to Lomax," she informed him, the prospect of progress infusing her plea with a renewed sense of purpose.

As Jeannie made her way to the hotel lobby, she found Ismail comfortably seated, savoring a steaming cup of coffee. He nodded towards an empty cup, offering it to her. "No offense, boss, but you look like crap. Did you sneak out of your room and hit some nightlife?" he quipped with a mischievous grin.

"I wish," Jeannie retorted, managing a wry smile. "Just another headache, and before you ask, I did take my pills for whatever good they're supposed to do. Lomax got another anonymous email. All it said was that the case is solved and that we just have to go to this address and wrap it up."

"Conceited bastard, isn't he?" Ismail remarked a hint of amusement in his voice. The camaraderie between the two, forged in the crucible of their shared challenges, allowed for banter that cut through the tension of their investigative pursuits. The hotel lobby became an informal arena for their exchange, a respite from the weight of the case they were about to close.

"Natalia, I must admit, Vincent D'Amico had quite the grand scheme in play," Delaney began, his tone carrying a blend of acknowledgment and incredulity. "Steal the relics, utilize artificial intelligence to craft convincing replicas, and then sell them to unsuspecting benefactors. A clever stratagem. And when they eventually realize they've been duped, you would be long gone, with both the loot and the authentic relics. Bravo."

As he spoke, there was a hint of admiration in Delaney's voice, an acknowledgment of the cunning intricacies woven into the elaborate plan. The room seemed to absorb the weight of the unmasking, the magnitude of the scheme revealing itself in the charged atmosphere between them. Natalia's involvement in this high-stakes game of deception became clearer, her role in executing D'Amico's audacious vision coming to light in the face of Delaney's revelations.

"By chance, did D'Amico ever explain the Cardinals' motivation to hire you to steal the relics? I mean, there had to be an ultimate goal, correct?" Delaney asked as Natalia was busy formulating a means of escape.

"Vincent wasn't the mastermind you make him out to be," Natalia asserted, her voice a blend of defiance and frustration. Her gaze shifted to Tim's lifeless form beside her, emphasizing her point. "Tim here was the brains of the outfit, especially when it came to handling the finances and bypassing those sophisticated alarm systems we had to overcome to steal those relics. Vincent was all fluff."

As she spoke, Natalia couldn't help but notice Tim's discarded gun in her peripheral vision. A spark of opportunity flickered in her eyes. If she could divert Delaney's attention, a swift escape with a well-aimed shot seemed within reach.

"Vincent might have had charisma, but Tim was the one who ensured the success of our operations," she continued, attempting to sow doubt in Delaney's mind. The room crackled with tension as the chess game between captor and captive played out, each move carrying the weight of potential consequences.

"The priests, or Cardinals, or whatever they fancy themselves, had a plan to break away from the Catholic Church in Rome," Natalia disclosed, her voice a blend of nonchalance and detached observation. She leaned back, a hint of a sardonic smile playing on her lips. "Their aim? To establish a new Church, one that clung fervently to traditional teachings. Frankly, we didn't give a damn about their motivations. As long as they paid for our services—and pay well they did—we were more than content to operate in the shadows, executing their clandestine requests."

Her casual tone belied the gravity of the information she was sharing. The room, charged with the echoes of conspiracy, seemed to tighten around the revelation. Natalia's words hung in the air, painting a picture of a covert alliance built on mutual interests, where morality took a backseat to financial gain.

Natalia, sensing an opportunity for escape, chose a moment when Delaney's attention wavered. With calculated precision, she allowed the sheet covering her nudity to slip to the ground, her movements a deliberate attempt to distract Delaney. In the brief seconds it took for the cloth to fall, her eyes locked onto Tim's discarded gun.

Seizing the chance, Natalia lunged toward the weapon, her fingers closing around its cold steel. The room held its breath as she prepared to raise it, the tension escalating with each passing heartbeat. However, before she could fully bring the gun to bear, Delaney, ever vigilant, reacted with swift, lethal precision.

Two sharp shots echoed through the room as Delaney, a sentinel in control, unleashed bullets that found their mark. Natalia's fleeting moment of defiance ended abruptly as the impact of the bullets sent shockwaves through her body. She stared at Delaney before falling onto the bed next to Tim. The room, a witness to this fatal dance, bore witness to the abrupt cessation of a dangerous game. The silence that followed was filled only with the weight of irrevocable choices and the lingering echoes of an ill-fated escape attempt.

Anticipating the unknown, Jeannie and Ismail opted for a rental car this time, arranging for its delivery at their location. The decision reflected the cautious uncertainty surrounding their destination.

As the compact vehicle pulled up, they wasted no time, trusting the GPS on Jeannie's cell to guide them to the mysterious location that awaited them.

Embarking on the journey, the GPS led them through a maze of winding roads, their headlights piercing the veil of darkness as the night grappled with the retreating shadows. Several hours passed before they reached a modest home nestled inconspicuously among businesses that still clung to closure, their façades silhouetted against the backdrop of a dawning day.

The small hours of the morning painted an eerie canvas, and the quiet streets amplified the suspense hanging in the air. The home, standing alone in the stillness, seemed to hold its secrets close. As Jeannie and Ismail approached, the creaking of the car's tires on the pavement echoed the hushed anticipation that enveloped the neighborhood.

Parking down the street, they watched but saw no activity, just a parked van on the curb near the residence. "Looks like one of the three vans that came out of the castle," Ismail said. "Must be the place."

"Something doesn't feel right," Jeannie said. "I'm going to sneak up on the van and see what is inside. Cover me." Jeannie got out of their rental and slowly closed the door to minimize the sound in the quiet surroundings.

Encountering a locked rear door of the van, Jeannie wasted no time. She deftly extracted a small flashlight from her jacket, its beam piercing through the darkness as she directed it into the window. The tinted glass offered only a partial view, revealing a large object within—a silhouette reminiscent of the Shroud of Turin, or so it seemed in her estimation. The enigmatic presence of such a significant artifact intensified the mystery shrouding the van.

Returning to the rental, Jeannie leaned back into the driver's seat and relayed her findings to Ismail. "I saw something in there, Ismail," she began, her voice hushed. "It's big, and from what I could make out, it looks like it might be something akin to the Shroud of Turin. We need to be cautious; this could be more significant than we initially thought." The weight of the revelation hung in the air, and the implications of their discovery sparked a surge of anticipation and trepidation.

"So, what's the next move?" Ismail inquired, his eyes reflecting a mix of uncertainty and readiness. "Do we reach out to the local authorities? Waiting for them could escalate things if the suspects are inside. It's a tricky situation. Good thing you're calling the shots, boss."

Down the street, perched discreetly with his sniper scope, Delaney observed the unfolding scenario, the distant figures of Jeannie and Ismail mere shadows in his lens. A wry smile crossed his face as he pondered the complexities of their predicament. "Damn if you do, and damn if you don't," he mused silently.

The weight of the decision lay squarely on Jeannie's shoulders.

"You'll have to make the call, Jeannie," he thought, his analytical mind acknowledging the delicate balance between action and restraint in this high-stakes situation. The street, caught in hushed suspense, became the stage for the impending choices that could either defuse or ignite the tension hanging in the air.

Sean observed Jeannie and Ismail emerging from their vehicle and moving stealthily toward the house with guns drawn. "We're on thin ice here, Ace," Jeannie whispered.

"Understood. Be careful," he replied.

"That's the way, Jeannie," Delaney muttered to himself as he monitored their approach, already anticipating what awaited them.

The duo advanced towards the front door. Ismail gestured that he would check the rear of the residence first. Upon his return, he informed Jeannie that the back door was locked and showed signs of recent use. Jeannie then pointed to the front door, and Ismail noticed it was partially open. With her small flashlight in hand, Jeannie pushed the door open further to catch a glimpse of the interior.

"Bodies," she said to Ismail. "At least three that I can see."

"Well, in the States, I would say we have more than enough probable cause," Ismail replied, preparing to head in right after Jeannie. Upon entering, they discovered all the dead crew members on the floor, some of whom were covered in vomit.

"Poison, I think," Jeannie said.

Ismail directed their attention toward the solitary bedroom. As they proceeded cautiously, an eerie silence enveloped the surroundings, devoid of any discernible sounds emanating from within. Ismail approached the closed door, his senses on high alert. Upon reaching for the handle, he discovered it was unlocked. He exchanged a quick glance with Jeannie, who nodded in acknowledgment.

"FBI!" Ismail shouted as he pushed the door open. The room unveiled a haunting scene—Natalia's lifeless form lay adjacent to Tim's, both clearly having succumbed to untimely demises. The stillness within the room mirrored the profound weight of the situation, leaving an indelible mark on the investigators as they absorbed the chilling reality before them.

As Ismail surveyed the bedroom scene, he remarked, "Don't see Vincent D'Amico."

Jeannie, deep in thought, added, "I suspect that Natalia here shot him in the Holy Sepulchre. It wouldn't surprise me if she wasn't the true mastermind behind all these thefts and finally decided it was time to take over as the leader."

Ismail's brows furrowed as he considered the implications. "If Natalia orchestrated this and eliminated D'Amico, we might be dealing with a whole new level of criminal sophistication. It's possible she saw an opportunity to seize control and capitalize on the chaos."

Jeannie nodded in agreement, her gaze fixed on the lifeless figures in the room. "We'll need to dig deeper into her connections, find out who might be pulling the strings from the shadows. This could be more than just a series of thefts; it might be part of a larger, more sinister plan."

As they delved into the complex web of motives and potential conspiracies, the investigators felt the weight of the situation intensify, realizing they were on the precipice of unraveling a mystery that extended far beyond a string of criminal acts.

CHAPTER THIRTY-TWO

Jeannie's fingers brushed against the cool metal of the keys on the nightstand next to the lifeless forms of Natalia and Tim. Leaving Ismail inside the house, she headed out to make a crucial call to Lomax, who had pressed her to disregard the time difference between Israel and San Francisco; Jeannie felt a sense of urgency mingled with curiosity. Her first objective was to explore the contents of the van, and if her suspicions held true, she planned to discreetly relock it, notifying the authorities that she had not breached its contents.

As she opened the van, her attention diverted momentarily to a medium-sized box tucked beside the container that she believed housed the Shroud of Turin. Intrigued, she unraveled the layers of bubble wrap until her fingers met an ancient relic—the True

Cross. In the dim light, she examined the artifact, its significance slowly revealing itself to her.

The weight of the True Cross in her hands evoked a profound connection, a sensation she couldn't quite articulate. The artifact seemed to resonate with something deep within her, an inexplicable link that transcended the boundaries of time and circumstance. Jeannie couldn't fathom the mystical forces at play.

Examining the intricate details of the True Cross illuminated by the beam of her flashlight, Jeannie mused, "Not much of a relic." Little did she realize that this seemingly unremarkable artifact held secrets that would weave into her own destiny in ways beyond her wildest imagination. Unbeknownst to her, the mystical forces embedded in the True Cross were poised to shape the course of her life in unforeseen ways.

Lost in thought, Jeannie found herself drawn to the ancient relic, and in a spontaneous, almost unconscious gesture, she pressed a kiss over the True Cross. The act, seemingly insignificant in the moment, carried with it an unspoken connection—a bond forged between her and the artifact that held mysteries waiting to be unraveled.

Skipping the Sudarium, Jeannie redirected her focus to the larger container, convinced it housed the revered Shroud. As she delicately peeled away a layer of foam rubber, the Shroud emerged, revealing the serene visage of the pursued Christ, His eyes peacefully closed. The intricacies of the image captivated her, each detail telling a story that spanned centuries.

Caught in the moment, the large van suddenly erupted out of the night with a rumble of thunder and the stark illumination of lightning streaking across the sky. The unexpected convergence of natural elements startled Jeannie, causing her to jump. The juxtaposition of the ancient relic before her and the elemental display outside created a surreal atmosphere as if the forces of nature were responding to the unveiling of a sacred artifact with their own dramatic performance.

Carefully restoring the foam rubber protection over the Shroud and rewrapping the True Cross, Jeannie secured the artifacts within the van before stepping out and methodically relocking it. With a sense of accomplishment, she reached for her phone and dialed Lomax, her anticipation growing with each ring until he finally answered on the third one.

"Jeannie, what's happening? Are you and Ismail okay?" Lomax's concern was palpable through the phone.

"We're both fine. The investigation has reached its conclusion, and I'm pleased to report that all three relics are now in our possession," Jeannie reassured him. She proceeded to provide a detailed account of the day's events, recounting the climactic discoveries they had made.

Lomax, processing the information, responded swiftly, "I'll get in touch with the State Department immediately. We need the Israeli authorities to take over from here and ensure the safe return of the relics. Simultaneously, I'll reach out to Interpol and expedite communication with the Vatican to prevent the relics from vanishing into the shadows. Just hold tight until I can get the Israeli police to respond and relieve you. Fantastic job."

As Jeannie concluded the call, a palpable mix of relief and anticipation lingered in the air. The intricate dance of international cooperation and swift action had been set into motion, aligning the gears that would ensure the safe return of the sacred artifacts to their rightful places. A sense of accomplishment enveloped Jeannie, knowing that the intricate diplomatic maneuvers she and Lomax had set in motion were paving the way for the relics to be safeguarded.

For reasons unknown, an unexpected craving surged within Jeannie, and she found herself drawn to the comfort of a Subway hot roast beef sub, accompanied by a side of potato chips and a refreshing Diet Dr. Pepper. Perhaps it was the culmination of the day's events that prompted this unusual desire, a need for sustenance amidst the weighty responsibilities they now shouldered.

The subsequent hours were consumed by a comprehensive interview with the Israeli authorities. The atmosphere was tense, yet a mysterious phone call received by the officer in charge seemed to tip the scales in their favor, expediting their release.

A subtle yet powerful force was at play, facilitating their interaction with an Interpol agent who, with a well-established rapport with the Israeli authorities, ensured their freedom. Soon, the pair found themselves making their way back to the hotel, the shadow of uncertainty gradually giving way to a sense of resolution.

Once they arrived back at their hotel, exhausted and famished, they decided to take advantage of the hotel's buffet before heading off to bed. Jeannie arranged their flights back to San Francisco the next morning.

The following morning, bathed in the soft glow of dawn, Jeannie and Ismail sat in a quiet corner of the hotel restaurant, sipping on their steaming cups of coffee. The ambiance was serene, a stark contrast to the intensity of the previous day's events. As they exchanged glances over the rims of their mugs, the entrance of three Cardinals caught their attention. Dressed in their distinctive crimson robes, the Cardinals conducted a brief survey of the room before making their way toward Jeannie and Ismail's table.

"Excuse us," Cardinal Mahoney spoke with a tone of dignified courtesy. "Are you the FBI agents who assisted in the capture of the three relics?"

Jeannie and Ismail nodded, acknowledging the Cardinals with a sense of curiosity. The Cardinals, representatives of the highest echelons of the Vatican, stood before them, their expressions a mix of gratitude and reverence. It was a surreal moment, the convergence of law enforcement and the ecclesiastical, a testament to the extraordinary nature of the relics they had helped recover. Apparently, they were unaware that the investigation of their involvement with Vincent D'Amico was still underway by the Vatican security force and Interpol.

As they engaged in conversation, the Cardinals expressed their heartfelt thanks, emphasizing the significance of Jeannie and Ismail's roles in securing these sacred artifacts. The intersection of worlds — the secular and the sacred — unfolded in that hotel restaurant as the Cardinals sought to convey the Vatican's profound gratitude for the successful resolution of a crisis that transcended borders and beliefs. They then excused themselves and left.

"Hmm, I wonder what's going to happen to them?" Ismail queried, a touch of curiosity in his voice.

"God knows," Jeannie replied with a wry smile, evoking a chuckle from Ismail. "I don't know about you, but I'm still hungry. I'm going back for seconds." She began to rise from her chair.

"Guess the headaches are gone?" Ismail remarked, a note of lightness in his tone as he followed Jeannie to the buffet table.

"You know, I forgot to take my pills before going to sleep, and I slept like a baby," Jeannie commented, her words carrying a lighthearted tone. Momentarily, she pushed aside the heavy reality of the fatal brain tumor she carried, aware that she only had perhaps four months left. The weight of her condition lingered beneath the surface as she recounted the restful night.

Acknowledging the impending need to check in with her doctor upon their return, as per his request, Jeannie found solace in the gratitude she felt. She silently thanked a higher power for granting her the time to unravel the enigma of the Relics of Redemption case. Amid her personal struggle, the successful resolution of the investigation provided a sense of purpose and accomplishment, allowing her to embrace each moment with a profound appreciation for the time she had been granted.

The levity in their exchange marked a shift from the weighty concerns of the investigation, signaling a return to normalcy that both agents welcomed. As they navigated the array of dishes, the uncertainty of the relics' fate was momentarily overshadowed by the simple pleasures of a shared meal and the camaraderie between two colleagues who had weathered a storm together.

OTHER BOOKS BY THE AUTHOR:

JEANNIE LOOMIS

Ark of the Covenant – Raid on the Church of Our Lady Mary of Zion

Star Chamber

Forgotten Plans

House of Special Purpose

Time Game

Thin Blue Line

The Fourth Reich

Black Heart/Black Cell

Phantom Train

Roller Coaster

Snow Angel

The Fourth Reich Reborn

HORROR BOOKS:

House on Haunted Hill Resurrection

Beneath the Earth

Carnival of Lost Souls

The Tingler Unleashed

SEAL – Ghost Recon

Christmas Novella:

The Hidden Workshop

NON-FICTION:

Toward the Integration of Police Psychology Techniques to Juvenile Delinquency in

K-12 Classrooms.

Teaching Inside the Walls

How to Create a Public-School Military-Style Book Camp Academy

AUTHOR'S BIBLIOGRAPHY

Meet Gary J. Rose, a former police sergeant from the Milpitas Police Department who transitioned into a passionate educator for at-risk incarcerated juveniles and adults post-retirement. Armed with a Ph.D. in social psychology, he embarked on a rewarding journey of instructing graduate students before eventually retiring.

Gary's literary journey took off with his debut novel, *Hitting Rock Bottom*, which quickly soared to Amazon's best-seller list. Inspired by his success, he introduced readers to the captivating FBI agent Jeannie Loomis, the central character in his thrilling series spanning thirteen gripping novels.

Exploring new literary horizons, Gary ventured into the world of horror novels, consistently achieving recognition in the top 10% of their respective genres. When he's not weaving stories, you can find him basking in the sun on the shores of Myrtle Beach, South Carolina, living his dream.

WHO IS FBI AGENT JEANNIE LOOMIS?

Jeannie Loomis is a committed yet imperfect agent in her forties working within the FBI. Her journey through the ranks took place during a time when the upper echelons of the bureau were predominantly male-dominated. Raised by deeply religious parents with a strong sense of patriotism, she continues to attend mass every weekend as a reminder of her upbringing.

Following the passing of her adoptive parents, Jeannie's pursuit of excellence propelled her to the role of Assistant Special Agent in Charge at the San Francisco FBI office. Her shielding from the agency's intricate politics is owed to her capable supervisor, Lomax, who holds the position of Special Agent in Charge.

Enduring the collapse of two marriages due to the strains of her demanding job, Jeannie found herself spiraling into a cycle of frequenting bars, often succumbing to heavy drinking and waking up beside unfamiliar partners. A tragic incident resulted in a pregnancy, which tragically ended in a violent confrontation at the substation where she was stationed.

Armed with a Ph.D. in psychology, Jeannie, along with her closest confidant and partner Ismail Flores, has been instrumental in a series of high-profile investigations, some of which remain concealed from public knowledge due to their sensitive nature. Uncovering the truth about her biological heritage following her birth mother's demise revealed a startling secret: Jeannie is a wealthy heir, a revelation she only recently disclosed to Flores.

Much like the famed fictional investigator Lucas Davenport, popularized by author John Stanford, Jeannie subscribes to the belief that achieving the greater good sometimes necessitates morally complex methods.

www.ingramcontent.com/pod-product-compliance
Lightning Source LLC
Chambersburg PA
CBHW020553310726
48979CB00008B/1202/J

* 9 7 9 8 9 8 9 3 4 2 4 4 0 *